Infidelity

Dejan Trajkoski

Infidelity

Translated from the Macedonian
by Paul Filev

DALKEY ARCHIVE PRESS
McLean, Illinois / Dublin, Ireland

Originally published as Неверство in 2014.
Copyright © by Dejan Trajkoski, 2014.
First Dalkey Archive edition, 2020.

CIP Data available upon request.

McLean, IL / Dublin

www.dalkeyarchive.com

Printed on permanent/durable acid-free paper.

Infidelity

The Narrator

A SILENT LUNAR dust descended over the earth that night with noble intent; like a gentle spray from a waterfall, the sparkling motes caressed the belly of the sweat-soaked woman, and the seed slid propitiously from her womb. Sunny came into being. His voice struck the air, his eyes perceived the radiance, his body sensed the closeness of another human being. Sunny, the child whose name was borrowed from the sun, began the eternal cycle of parting and reunion. That night the Fates, from whose decrees there is no escape, said:

May this child's eyes radiate tenderness and firmness like those of a holy icon. The second one said: may both calm and turbulent winds be his companions; may he sport with them as though with brothers. The third one said: may he discover all the colors of the spectrum, may he combine them, may he have the power to see even the tear of the queen bee; and may he search farther and deeper, in the shadow of a dream, and in the dirty rains.

And so it came to pass. In summer he was visited by snow, and in winter sweltering heat. Like all travelers.

*

Sunny had many journeys in life. The first and most important for him began when his young eyes, which had yet to sense a different kind of gaze, fluttered and trembled from the closeness of Luna, the girl whose name was borrowed from the moon. Another began when he boarded a ship.

Sunny

THE HEAVY ANCHOR delivered a parting kiss to the seabed, and we set sail. How we all managed to get on board the ship even I don't know. One way or another, we were shoved head over heels down below, down to the very bottom, into the darkness, piled up against one another as if we were a stack of kindling, freshly cut from the woods, loaded onto a donkey, and tightened securely with a rope so we couldn't move, so we wouldn't make any trouble.

That night somehow we managed to lie down. But I neither slept nor dreamed. I just lay there, and in the muffled chorus of sleepy voices, I sifted through flashes of my departure from Macedonia for America. I didn't understand those first dreamlike visions in the belly of that giant sea monster. All I know is that the ship transformed into something else, something equally huge, but above all impalpable—like my father's shoes, one size too big, which often carried him home much later than they should, when all the knobbly logs in the fireplace had burned out and the house had become as cold as a tomb; or his hunting rifle, which he paid more attention to than to my mother, who lay awake waiting for him to come home, stroking us gently as we slept. Those gentle strokes often woke me. But when I grew up a bit, around the age of eight or nine, I didn't push her hand away. Instead, I let her stroke me, because we all have a need to be human and to feel something human; and my mother was human, deeply human.

Naturally, every night while traveling on the ship, I reawakened Luna in my heart, the girl with the liveliest eyes, with the most remarkable name, whose hands were covered in needle pricks from threading tobacco, and were blackened by the muddy leaves, a mud that can't be washed or scraped off, and that remains on the person the whole summer long as the obligatory mark of poverty bestowed on the people who live in my parts.

4

I first saw her when her family moved to our town from their village. In a dress reaching to the ground, the bottom of which was lined with mud, and wearing two different sandals. She was staring at my piece of baked bread smeared with pork fat and sprinkled with red pepper finely ground by the patient and gnarled hands of my grandmother, who could pick out a sweet pepper from a bitter one and extract the tiniest motes of dust from it, just like a fairy godmother.

"Can I have a bite?" she asked.

I don't know if she was smiling or not. I handed her the piece of bread, which she nibbled as if sampling one of the pastries that I stood before years later, staring at them through the shop windows in New York, thinking twice before parting with the money to buy one, a chocolate one, with a dollop of whipped cream and a cherry, a red cherry on top, like those we used to steal from our neighbors' yard when we were small.

Luna chewed on the bread and stared straight into my eyes, without saying a word. My cheeks flushed hot.

"Do you know what my name is?" she asked.

"No," I said, in a voice that didn't seem to belong to me.

"It's Luna. I've got an unusual name. And yours?"

"Sunny," I said.

"You have an unusual name too. And you're quite red in the face. Do you have a temperature?" she asked.

"No," I answered briefly, as though frightened, lowering my eyes, and stealing a glance to see whether my face really was red.

"Let's have a look. My mother puts her hand on my forehead to see if I have a temperature," she said.

She pressed her hand against my forehead, holding it there for some time. I looked into her eyes and felt scared. I don't know what made me take fright, and I began looking up instead of at her.

"You have a temperature," she said.

"Can I have another bite," she asked, and before I could reply, half the piece of bread was gone. She handed back the other half, and ran off home . . .

And so, after exchanging only a few words with her, Luna became the girl who made my tongue go dry for the first time, made it go numb, made it prick as though stung with nettles— and not just because of the image of her as a child holding a piece of bread in her hand, which had struck me at the time. The next day I asked my grandmother to make some more of that bread. She rolled her sleeves up higher, which she kept rolled up all winter and summer long—because old age brings on chills or hot flashes, depending on a person's constitution, she used to say—and placed my future hopes for another encounter on the woodstove, while I ran to the outhouse because, even out of sight, Luna made my stomach churn from fear, or rather from something far more confusing, which I didn't have a name for at the time. I didn't see Luna for three days after that. I threw down three pieces of bread in front of her gate, just farther up our street. On the fourth day I saw her. We were playing marbles. She stopped to watch. I didn't look at her. Out of fear. After a short while she left. That night I fell asleep with my head in my grandmother's lap. I regret not being able to recall my exact thoughts at the time, but I know that I'd never been happier, not even when my father took me hunting for the first time—the first and only time in my childhood—together with my neighbor Kole, and the two of us howled like wild hounds throughout the mountain to frighten the wild animals, to force the wild boar they were pursuing to run past us, so they could take its life with their rifles, which they also let us hold in our hands. That was the first time I ever felt close to my father, a feeling of closeness that quickly left me whenever he felt the need to go to the tavern.

The Narrator

HUMANS ARE THE loneliest creatures on earth. When they're born, the first to pay them a visit is loneliness; it nestles down in the scar of the navel, like a vile disease. Next comes pain, the origin of the first infant cry. Only after that does a person become acquainted with joy, which is cousin to comfort. The game is played between those four unequal forces.

Sunny

I COULD THINK about Luna from here to the moon and back, longer than all the rivers and streams I've ever run down put together. And our entire history together always flashes across my mind like a short newsreel—which I saw for the first time when I went abroad—like the hundreds of frames in a film-strip, countless hundreds and thousands that last only a short time in comparison to the considerable effort that goes into their production. From that abridged but essential version what comes back to me is the autumn following the summer with the pieces of bread, that unjust time for us who were living in Macedonia at the beginning of the second decade of the twentieth century, which, later on, drove me to leave home in order to have something, as my folks said, or to have nothing in order to have something, as I said at the beginning. Be that as it may . . . Ultimately, all times are unjust, and the one in which we live is always the most unjust.

For a short period of time we went to school, where they taught us that two and two are four, although later on I learned that that's the case only for the poor. We all studied together, gathered up like bales of hay, crammed side by side like prickly stalks of straw. The teacher often rapped me on the hand with a stick, because, as he'd say, my mind wandered off with the birds outside. I couldn't see what was so wrong with my mind wandering off, not just with the birds, but also with the trees that seemed to vie with one another to see which would be the greenest; or with the neighborhood dogs, counting their barks, and wondering what they were saying to each other.

"Ow, ow—I'm hungry," the puppy said to its father. "Woof, woof, woof—Tell your mother," the father said. "Owf, ow, aow, aoow," whined the puppy sweetly, telling its mother, "Mom, I'm hungry Mom," and the mother probably licked the puppy, and gave it something to eat. That's what I imagined the dogs and the wolves talked about at night, in the harsh winters when they wound their way down from the nearby hills, threatening

8

to break into the warm henhouses, waiting for naughty children to be brought to them, as our parents used to say to frighten us into behaving. No other living creature—neither the birds nor the chickens nor the kittens—spoke. I don't know why.

Luna was the most beautiful girl in school, not just on our street. Everyone liked her, and that didn't sit well with me. She began hanging out with Fima, a quiet girl who lived a bit farther down the road from us. Until I started school, I had only seen Fima walking past our house. At the time, I didn't even know her name. She wasn't very pretty, but neither was she unattractive. She seemed strange somehow, with sharp features, imposing, and at times you might even say a bit scary looking. After school, I walked home together with Fima, Luna, Vlado, Damjan, Kiro, and Stojanče. One time a dog started barking, and Fima said: "It wants to go out for a walk." The blood in my veins froze. Fima also plays at imagining what dogs say, I thought to myself, just like me! I hated her after that because it was she, and not Luna, who played my favorite game. Every time she asked me something, I always replied gruffly to her, the way I did to my brother whenever he took my last cookie and shoved it whole into his mouth, mumbling: "If you tell on me, I'll pull your ears like a donkey." Then he'd laugh, spraying crumbs from the cookies made of flour and lard and sprinkled sparsely with sugar. Luna was always talking to Fima and never had any time leftover to ask me anything. And I waited for her. I waited every day for her to ask me something really important that I'd know the answer to, that I'd know the answer to better than anyone else in school, so that she could see that I'm the best, better at everything than any of the others, and then after that, she'd only want to talk to me because no one else knows things the way I do! That was my problem, at the time bigger than all the problems of the cosmos, although the adults used to say: "You kids don't have a worry in the world, you've got it good." Not that things weren't good for me; they both were and weren't, because Luna hardly seemed to notice me. And even when she did, it was simply to ask me if I'd be walking back home with them.

"C'mon Sunny, we're going home, what are you waiting for," she'd say to me, and I'd run after them like the snot-nosed kid that, in reality, I was.

One day, Luna fell ill. She didn't come to school for almost a whole month. All us neighborhood kids went to see her. Those who could, brought her a little something to eat. Vlado brought her a piece of white bread, a jar of green fig preserve, and a jar of black fig preserve. His family was the most well off and that's why Vlado was the fattest kid. The preserves were in small jars. Vlado asked her to give back the jars when they finished the jam, and to make sure they were washed, he said, that's what his mother had told him. Auntie Stojanka—Luna's mother—hesitated for a moment, as if debating whether to take the gifts.

"Well then, we'll make sure to wash them. God forbid we return them unwashed," she said.

Kiro brought her some grape preserve, the kind without seeds that I liked best of all, and that made my mouth water as soon as I saw it. I didn't see what the others brought because Luna spoke to me personally, me first is what I mean. She fixed her gaze on me and I froze, thinking to myself, I'll show my true colors now, she'll see how special I am. And I stared at her mouth to see what kind of sweet words would emerge from it, and I waited in that moment that seemed longer than my entire childhood, I waited with fear and trepidation, so in love and terrified that even today I don't know how my young heart managed to withstand such strong emotions, and she said: "Sunny, why are your cheeks so red? And why didn't Fima come?"

My whole world came crashing down, like so many other times before. I crumbled instantly, the way my grandmother sometimes does, shedding a tear or two for no apparent reason, without warning, the tears sliding down her face as smooth as that of a young girl's instead of an old woman's.

"I'm not red," I said, "and Fima . . ." My voice caught, as though choked with emotion, preventing me from becoming the most important boy in her world, of becoming the hero of our street with whom everyone wanted to play.

"I don't know about Fima, but well, I—I—I came . . ." I stuttered, and my face fell, as if the redness from my cheeks had dragged it down, as if it had melted and slid down like a drop of water from a rain-soaked leaf. So much for all that. So much for my expectations that she'd ask me something she had never asked anyone else before, and that I'd respond with something so important, something so incredibly important, that afterward everyone would see me as someone important, the way I saw Pere the little ruffian as someone important. Instead, I sat there with cheeks flaming, feeling as though my whole childhood was fading away, as though my whole youthful future and all my dreams were fading away, including the hope of proving to my father that I wasn't a snot-nosed brat, something that he had called me on numerous occasions.

We stayed a bit longer. Her parents asked us to tell them what we'd learned in school, and Vlado told them how the teacher had fallen asleep in class and how everyone had laughed.

"Damjan and I chucked a peach pip at him and he woke up, but he didn't see it," Vlado laughed as he recounted the story, and everyone else laughed too, including Luna, and I hated Vlado, because they were laughing with him, and not with me. After that, Damjan said that his parents made dogberry preserve and black plum preserve and quince preserve and cherry preserve too, with the cherries from the tree in their yard, which was the same tree we secretly stole cherries from, while his grandmother chased us away, yelling: "May lightning strike you for stealing, you little swine! If I catch any of you, I'll teach you a lesson." And then Damjan told us not to steal their cherries because there'd be a lot less preserve for him.

"But you can steal some if you want to, because you're not well," he said to Luna, and everyone burst out laughing once again. All except me. And as if that weren't enough, Luna asked me another question:

"Sunny, why aren't you laughing?" which finished me off completely. No reply sprang to my young brain, no words came to my mouth clamped shut, time was ticking past, the room fell silent, all eyes on me, until Vlado said:

"Cat's got his tongue." Laughter erupted once again, and I saw myself as if from on high, from above, as though witnessing myself shrink down to the size of an ant.

"We can take you home if you're not feeling well," said Auntie Stojanka.

I said I was fine, and stood up and left.

Auntie Stojanka didn't even see me out. I think her mind was on the preserves. So much so that I think she could hardly wait for us all to leave so they could eat them. That afternoon I lay down and put my head in grandmother's lap. She was knitting. She stroked my head gently, and told me she had work to do, that she had to get up. I told her that I wanted to lie down for a bit with my head on her lap, and she told me not to get mad because her work wouldn't wait for her. She left the room, and with her, at the same time, seemingly all hope was gone, because when a child feels shattered by the pain of young love, as I did that day, then all problems seem greater, even greater than the forced separation of two adults in love. It didn't help, either, when she appeared momentarily at the door, saying that she'd be back right away. To top it all off, my mother was gently stroking my brother's head, who, like Luna, was also unwell. My father wasn't at home. I lay curled up in a ball, waiting for my grandmother so I could lie down beside her, across her lap, which was a form of consolation for all the pain of childhood, but which later on in life just seems silly and even naïve. That night I didn't even have her lap to comfort me—my grandmother didn't return to the room until much later. I had never been so sad before.

The next day Fima wanted to know if Luna had asked about her. I said: "Why don't you go ask her yourself?" She said: "My father wouldn't let me come, so I wouldn't get infected. Did you get infected?" "No," I said, but at that moment I wished I had gotten sick, so I could be lying down ill, like Luna, and have her come visit me, and she would tell me how school had been, and then I would ask her something, I would ask her something instead of waiting for her to ask me. That's what I thought to myself. And I felt much happier than the night before. Then, for the next two weeks, Fima and I walked home from school together.

The following day, I don't know where my unexpected courage came from, but I openly asked her:

"What's that dog saying?"

"He's calling to his son. He's saying, 'it's time to come home, it's time for dinner,'" she said, and smiled. She even asked me:

"What's the puppy saying now?"

"It's saying: 'no way—we're in the middle of playing a game; spread some jam on a bit of bread, and bring it down to me here on the street,'" I said, and we erupted in a fit of laughter.

Fima and I laughed every day during those two weeks, every day, not just on the way home from school, but also during the breaks between classes. We became such close friends that all the boys said I was a sissy, which I took quite hard, and I told my mother about this right away, but I also told her not to tell my father. I wanted to say to her, tell the other mothers to tell their kids not to call me that, but I didn't say that to her. Then Luna returned, and suddenly, as though a magic wand had been waved, everything went back to the way it was before she'd fallen ill.

"What's the dog saying now, Sunny," Fima asked me as we were all heading home together. I looked at her reproachfully, with angry eyes, like Uncle Momo's the time he came to our place and asked my father to fetch him the thin wooden rolling pin so he could teach somebody how bread is made, and I thought happily to myself that my father would bring home some bread that night, some warm bread, and that he might give me some from the middle, from the soft white center that my grandmother sometimes gave us when she took the bread out of the oven, with steam still escaping from it, digging her remaining teeth into the crust, and saying: "Oh, oh, glorious bread, more precious than a living soul." But as I was saying, I glared at Fima with angry eyes, and said to her:

"It's saying, 'mind your own business.'" That's what I said to her, like my father said to my mother.

For a long while after that everything was the same. Until I began to see Luna less and less. Her parents stopped sending her to school so she could help at home.

"At home she'll learn how to work—what'll she learn at school? When her husband comes home at the end of the day, will she greet him with a notebook? He's going to want food, not books," her father had said, and his word was law that no force could contravene. After that I also wanted to stop going to school, and the dogs stopped talking to each other.

The Narrator

SOME YEARS LATER there came a big drought. It was a summer like no other, when even the ants forgot what dew was. Not a single drop of moisture hung from the tips of the grass blades so the ants might quench their thirst. The wretched drought devastated everything, making even the trees in the fields sad, making them droop, leaving them bent halfway to the ground, like orphans. At the time people said: "Even the sky has it in for us, dammit. It doesn't feel like pissing down to give us a good soaking, to let just a few precious drops fall." Others said: "God is horrified at everyone's wickedness, that's why he's not sending us any rain now. Later on he'll send us a flood, a great flood to clean up the evil from this land." And someone else said: "I've experienced both plenty and scarcity. I'm the child of an old mother, but I've never seen anything like this before. It must be something we've done wrong for there to be no mercy, as if it were only we who have sinned."

That summer, just as the Fates had decreed, and no differently, Sunny was visited by all four seasons.

Sunny

THAT WAS THE summer when I became fully conscious of my manhood, and Luna of her feminine assets. However, the times and the places were such that nobody dared do anything forbidden, not even in their thoughts, despite the fact that everyone at one time or another has committed all sorts of acts in their mind, the way people probably all over the world do, regardless of whether it's right or wrong or forbidden or that anyone even cares one way or another. At that time, the woods were the only witness to my desire, which in my mind took me to all the possible places of delight, undressing Luna, and leaving her as naked as the day she was born, as the saying goes, so entirely naked in my mind's eye that, even though I'd only known her a short time, I felt as though I were breathing in her smell. I wanted to bring her a bunch of flowers, to bring her all the flowers of the world, to swamp her with bouquets, to adorn her with every possible color and form. And I let her image rest in my mind a while longer, after the juices of my swollen manhood and desire had been spent, wondering whether she, too, felt the same desire.

My walks through the woods became more frequent. My grandmother was pleased when I brought her back different herbs, from which she made teas and remedies, some of which worked while others just made us nauseous. She always said that the plants I brought her were the very ones she needed.

"Oh my child, geraniums and pheasant's eye, they're just what I needed. And here you've brought me some anemones, marigolds, and fenugreek, Granny's precious little boy," she said, listing their names day after day: violet, rose and carnation, basil and iris, hyacinth, amaranth, xeranthemum, hellebore, tansy, goosegrass, wood fern, geranium, red bryony, lemon balm and dandelion, chamomile, St. John's Wort, yarrow, strawberry, cupid's dart, restharrow, wormwood . . . after which she secretly threw them out in the trash . . .

By then I had forgotten my childish fears (if it's true that they can be forgotten), the ones that had assailed me at the age

16

of ten or eleven, at those times when I feigned being asleep to listen to my parents talk about the things that children weren't supposed to hear. In my flights into the adult world I learned that Uncle Petse—Luna's father—beat Auntie Stojanka every day, and that apparently she once said she couldn't take it anymore, that she would go back to her mother's place in the village, after which Uncle Petse said to her: "So you want to go back to your mother's to badmouth me, you goddamned fucking bitch. Listen here, you set one foot out that door and not even St. Peter will be able to bring you back, you goddamned bitch. You'll see just how easy it is to cry even without a beating." That's what my grandmother said, chuckling as she recounted it, and I was glad that my father didn't beat my mother, but I began to fear that Auntie Stojanka might go back to her mother's village and take Luna with her. After that, at night, I clasped my hands together, squeezed my eyes tight, and, until I fell asleep, incessantly repeated, as an entreaty: "Please don't let Luna leave, please don't let Luna leave, please don't let Luna leave . . ."

I also overheard that in some city—"Bucharest" my father called it, somewhere far away—someone signed an agreement. I didn't understand what that was, but he said: "It's got so as you can't tell who's going to give you a rifle, goddamn 'em, whether it'll be the Serbs, the Bulgarians, and all of 'em just waitin' to clobber us. Now listen woman, if they take me as a soldier, you go back to your parents' village, cover up the cellar to conceal it, and hide down there with the children if you hear anyone approach." I prayed then that we wouldn't go to the village, and I repeated to myself: "Please don't let us go to the village, please don't let us go to the village, please don't let us go to the village . . ." I said nothing about them taking my father away. I didn't let myself think about that possibility. Although, deep down, I sometimes prayed they'd take him, and then immediately after that I'd say to myself two or three times:

"Please don't let them take him, please don't let them take him," out of fear that someone could read my mind.

I once heard my grandmother say to my mother:

"Dear child, you were born to endure hardships, like all women, but heed your husband while he's still at home, because, after all, it's a lot worse to be alone than to have someone yelling at you every day." I didn't understand that.

But getting back to what I was saying, so as not to stray too far from what I wanted to say, one night, after repeating "please don't let us go to the village" and "please don't let Luna leave," I fell asleep, when suddenly a strange sound woke me. I opened one eye and saw my mother sitting on top of my father, jumping up and down on him. With bare, naked feet. She moaned a couple of times, the way I did when I had a high temperature. I closed my eyes at once, and heard my father say: "Quieter, you'll wake the children," and my mother let out a heavy sigh, as if something had broken inside her. That sound rang in my ears a long time—in my ears and in my fragile soul, unprepared for such a sight. The next day I swore to myself that I'd never grow up. And I pushed my mother's hand away every time she tried to stroke me. Overjoyed, she would say:

"Lord, Lord, how my boy's grown, it's got so as no one can even touch him anymore." What's more, I told everyone to turn around and close their eyes when I was getting undressed to take a bath, and the only person I allowed to bathe me was my grandmother, and then only while I was wearing my underpants. I argued with my parents because I didn't want to go to bed, so they took me to various holy men they'd heard of. Apparently the devil had got a hold of me and had cast some sort of evil spell over me, that's what they said, and he wouldn't let me sleep. They stopped searching for a cure for me when I told my mother to stop sleeping beside my father, or beside me. Then my anger subsided, my young soul somehow found a little shelter, and little by little I began to go to bed on time.

Ah, that was long ago . . . Everything is forgotten and nothing is forgotten. The way I never forgot Luna's tear, that tear that rolled down her cheek like a twin drop, as though shed mutually by us. And the way I had forgotten how many times I waited for Luna to open her sweet young mouth to utter the longed for words, to say the thing that would lift me off the ground, that would give wings to the most important boy in her life.

Everything I'd ever wanted to happen took place that summer, when the childhood traumas had already long faded. Then Uncle Petse began to beat Luna. Often she didn't know why. Quite simply, attractive physical traits were obstacles for women at that time. It set them apart, drawing the attention of all, and, for the fathers, this was forbidden, the ultimate sin, even though their own eyes often wandered over the other nubile bodies around them.

Luna and I rarely met up. And when we did, I didn't know what to say to her. Every second with her was torture. Her presence made my throat dry and my courage deserted me, even though before each meeting I tried to think of exactly what I would say to her, down to the smallest detail, right up to the moment when I would look her straight in the eye without fear, and wait for something out of this world to happen. Things went on like that until the day she showed up with a huge bruise over her eye. Then the sky darkened, a shadow crossed my brow, all the tremors of the earth shook me, and I told her:

"One day, I'm going to beat up your father."

Our twin tear rolled down her cheek, and on it, inscribed in capitals, was everything that I wanted her to tell me and me her, my whole life. Then Luna turned around and ran off again. After that I didn't see her for three days. I circled her house hundreds of times, and cast hundreds of wishes at her doorstep. I sent them off to sneak up beside her, to steal upon her like a little elf, to comfort her sorrow. That's how our true love began, which at the time, at the beginning of the twentieth century in Macedonia and in the Balkans, and even farther afield, didn't have a name.

The Narrator

LET'S SHIFT BRIEFLY over to the town's tavern, to see what Mitre and Petse—Sunny's and Luna's fathers—the innkeeper Mandža, and the priest are discussing.

"Even the sky has it in for us, dammit. It doesn't feel like pissing down to give us a good soaking, to let just a few precious drops fall, if nothing else. Well, what d'you reckon, Father, what does your God have to say? Why doesn't he send us a bit of rain to wash away all the filth that's gathered over this land, eh?"

"Who knows? Maybe he's fed up with such sinners, and he's just thinking to himself 'let 'em rot.'"

"I wasn't asking you, Petse."

"Uh-oh, the fighting cocks have gathered again. A glass of wine for you, Father?"

"Yes, yes, wine. But make it white. Red's too heavy at this time of day."

"Hey Father, if red wine is God's blood, then what's white wine—or should I rather say yellow? Ha, ha, ha. Hey Mitre, do you know? Or you, innkeeper? Eh? Ha, ha, ha."

"Oh, stop it man, I'm gonna piss myself laughing. Dammit, you know only too well what it is. Oh, you've made me split my sides, hee, hee, hee. I'm gonna spill this jug of wine from laughing if you don't stop."

"It depends on the individual, Petse, that's what this priest's got to say. It depends on what angle he sees it from."

"What d'you mean 'it depends,' Father? So in other words, what you're saying is, it's one thing for you and another for me?"

"Yes and no. All things of God are one and the same everywhere. It depends on how the individual looks at them and how he sees them. For me, everything is God's spirit—from the earth that the grapes sprouted from, to the wine in your glass. To you the grapes may just be grapes, and the wine just piss. It depends on the individual."

"Well, Father, I can see straight off that you're a learned man. The way you talk, a man could be excused for not understanding you, dammit! But then, let me bring you some wine. After all, you're a good soul."

"Yes, I can talk, but who knows for how long. You see, they all just come here and tell us what to do, what to call ourselves. They take the words out of our mouths and plant new ones in them. They want us to lament our name, to bury our bones under a different sky, to convert us, to rename our gravestones. That's what they want, the Bulgarians, the Serbs, the Greeks, all of them. And we don't have the strength to get our own back on them. But if you ask me, you know what we should do?"

"C'mon, Father, leave it alone. I'm not interested in prattling on about politics."

"No you're not, no you're not. None of you are. But that's what'll seal our doom. We'll seal our own doom, all hating one another in this way."

The Narrator

AS THE FATES decreed, the time came when Sunny began to discover all the colors of the spectrum. But he had yet to combine them.

Sunny

AFTER OUR TWIN tear, which hung suspended for a long time, sliding down not over a cheek but, instead, over the threshold of our unrevealed feelings, came the sense of anticipation. Everything was the same again, and yet nothing was the same. My throat went dry, my words fled far from the place where they were conceived, and I lowered my frightened eyes, imagining her lips instead of gazing longingly at them. Until Luna came up to me one day, her whole being drawing close to mine; as if two mountains had ripped loose from their eternal moorings, that's what the force of our attraction seemed like to me. And suddenly she kissed me on the cheek, swiftly and firmly, as a sickle cuts corn. And then she turned around again and ran off like a quick breeze, like a leaf sent flying by an autumn storm. But this time the storm subsided. Luna stopped as though rooted to the spot, standing there with her back toward me for what seemed like eternity, as near and as far as a mountain. She turned to face me, took a few uncertain steps, and with her gaze rooted to the ground said: "I don't know why I just did that. Don't tell anyone or my father will kill me." And then she went off again.

When I got back home, I recalled the story my grandmother once told my mother. The story about a woman who, after waiting ten years for her husband to return from working abroad, converted to Islam, and ran off with an Ottoman bey to become his Muslim wife. A few years later, however, the Turks left Macedonia; after five hundred years of Ottoman rule in Macedonia, the Turks departed. The woman could not have foreseen such an event. Who could have known, who would have believed, that after five centuries it would all come to an end? And precisely when it needn't have! The way it's hard to imagine that a love stronger than time will ever end. The bey, however, didn't take his Muslim wife with him to Turkey. The beautiful woman was left without him. Soon after that her husband returned. Her beauty was long gone from the thrashings she received from her husband's brothers, but her husband finished her off. They kicked her down the streets, her face covered in fresh scars, slashed with a knife that belonged to her husband, whom no one had ever asked how he had spent those ten years in America, how he had satisfied his desire for female flesh. Her suffering wasn't just at the hands of her loved ones; whoever approached her spat in her face, as if all five centuries of Ottoman oppression had accumulated entirely within her. They called her every name under the sun: "Slut, Turkish whore. May God curse you with rotten luck. May you regret the day you were born, you tramp. So you enjoyed it over there with the bey, eating Turkish delight and baklava, eh? Well here you are now, eat some dirt. Go on, eat it, swallow it, you slut," they said to her, and they filled her mouth with dirt. What didn't they do to her . . . She's become a beggar now. She ran off to Sofia. That's what they say, said my grandmother.

All that took place around the time I was born. Almost twenty years later, a kiss between two un-united bodies before the Great God was still forbidden in these parts. Not only was it forbidden, it was something you weren't even permitted to think about, even though, as I said, everyone thought about it, while some were even obsessed with it, a growling desire that plagued their minds. The kiss that Luna gave me was a cardinal sin. I would even go so far as to say that killing your own brother wouldn't have been as big a sin as kissing an unmarried woman at that time. But that night I was smiling like never before. My father burst through the door, anger plastered across his face, berating me for not having worked in the fields, complaining that nothing had been sown the way it should have been, and who knows what else. That night, for the first time I think, my father's words just bounced off me rather than entering me.

The Narrator

IT IS WRITTEN that people sometimes change the meanings of words. In such cases, when summer is winter, and winter late autumn, as the Fates decreed, it may happen that everything just fizzles out, that it doesn't take place, or else ensues like a torrid flood, tempestuous and fertile as the first spring kiss between the bee and the flower.

Sunny

FOR A LONG time after that, uncountably long, everything was the same again, even though nothing was the same. Until the day when the sun exploded like an over-ripe pumpkin, its blazing heat keeping everyone indoors, in the shade, while we, communing in silent accord, went off without a word to the nearby woods, separately so that no one would see us, and together the way only we two saw each other. From that time on, her eyes, blue like no others, looked at me differently from everything else. I could have given her everything on a silver platter or nothing at all; either way, it made no difference. A great devotion was born in Luna, the girl whose name was borrowed from the moon, with her snakelike hips, and breasts like two white rocks, which on washing days at the river spilled out of their secret hiding place, wrapped tight by the mothers so that misfortune would not visit them, as they said, or a secret delight, as the girls craved. The time of merely stealing glances at them came to an end almost at once; the river was no longer my sole means to have Luna as a woman, to have her for real, and not just secretly from afar, as I did before the kiss, and before our joint visits to the woods.

I doubt my mother noticed anything different about my eyes, that I was absent even when present. However, my grandmother was almost certainly able to see what can't be seen, after which she stroked me more tenderly than in the days when she used to comfort me as a child, only this time with words instead of with her rough hands:

"Son, should I tell your mother to look for a bride for you? You're not young anymore. What do you say? I see the time is ripe for Luna too . . ." I didn't hear anything else she said after that, and in the middle of her speech, I just squeezed her tightly the way she used to cuddle me as a child. My grandmother set about her business, and then one night my father came home, shook the unhappiness from his face—momentarily—and called to my mother, who, without being asked to, filled up his flask, and just stood there waiting for him to say all kinds of unnecessary things, as was his usual wont.

"Your little rascal's time has come. Send my mother out to find him a wife, and let her ask them for her hand. But as for money—I have none to give; and cattle, chickens, and that sort of thing—even less so. Let her offer them what paltry items we have as a dowry, and if they're prepared to hand her over like that, then let them do it. Your son can take care of feeding her after that; his hands aren't big and strong for nothing," he said to my mother, who at that moment experienced both joy and sorrow at the same time, as was her fate in life, while for the first time a dark, invisible tear that always seemed to poke at her eye rolled down her prematurely lined face.

In keeping with the way things were done, first off a matchmaker had to be found. That was usually someone close to the two families, someone who knew them well, who would know what to say, and who would do the necessary sweet-talking. My grandmother immediately chose Mara, the woman who had assisted her at two of her own deliveries—once even while she was working in the fields—and who, afterward, referred to the children as her own. "Ah, in those days women gave birth in the fields, and then carried on with their digging so it wasn't left unfinished. It wasn't like it is now," my grandmother would say, and I would laugh at her, telling her that she knew nothing about babies, who were delivered by stork. Mara was a well-known matchmaker, and it was said that if she set foot in someone's house, not only would the parents immediately hand over their daughter, but, you could also say, the bride and groom would become as one—that's how happy the couple would be if she were the one to arrange the marriage. But it was also said that, afterward, Mara would go over to the newlyweds' place nonstop and become an annoyance to them, eating them out of house and home, and at the same time saying: "Ah, if not for me, I doubt you'd be as happy as you are." But my grandmother told me not to worry, that if Mara started flapping her gums, she'd scald her with hot water like a chicken before it gets plucked.

So one Friday evening, according to custom, Mara came to our house because she had to set off from there, that's how it was done. My father placed an ax on the doorstep for Mara to jump over, so that her words would be as sharp as a blade. My father had spent a great deal of time sharpening the ax the previous day . . . My grandmother lit a fire even though it was hot, and spat three times into it, so the girl would sizzle with passion for the young man like the spit in the flame. I was drenched in sweat from that fire. My father was also sweating, but he didn't say anything. My mother tipped out a glass of water behind Mara as she was leaving, so her words would flow like a stream. Mara jumped over the ax, turned around, and said:

"You lucky devil, Sunny! Just wait and see what kind of bride I bring you back, may God grant her twins before long." Then my grandmother scolded her for turning around, saying she shouldn't have done that because things would go wrong, while Mara insisted to her that things would only go wrong if she had reentered the house, pointing out to her that she had merely turned around. And she told my grandmother not to babble on so much—that's what she said to her—because she knew her own work. At any rate, the matchmaker, enticed by the new pair of shoes that she'd be given for her services—as was the custom in those days—and by the thought of all the deep obeisances she'd receive at the wedding—where the matchmaker is sometimes even more important than the best man—went off to meet with Luna's parents, who were even poorer than we were and who, naturally, wouldn't hear of their daughter—the most beautiful girl, raised on corn and gruel and a drop of sunflower oil—going off to live in another wretched dump, about which they had no idea it needn't be so wretched just because it was a dump.

And so, there you have it. That's how it was that fate drove me aboard a ship in search of something that would carry me far away from Luna, and that would bring me back to her when time had gone by and carried off everything we should have experienced, but hadn't.

Before I left, it was both the happiest and the unhappiest time for me and for her; a time in which we cursed a fate that denied us the chance to be what we were.

It was the happiest time because Luna and I rebelled. We were defiant in a way that would have been inconceivable to ordinary people, to those who followed the well-trodden path of tradition, one, such as it was, that was predicated on a false sense of honesty and justice, as well as a false sense of belief and respect, and not the betrayal of one's individual desires, which must remain sacred, which must never be disclosed, because they didn't accord with the rules, rules that had plunged thousands of people into deep depression, born of unfulfilled drives. For me and for Luna, that defiance, not apparent to others, took us places where people seldom went. We got to know each other, to explore one another, and to become familiar with the most intimate details of our bodies. We left the cattle to graze, letting them follow their own whims and desires, while we entered without shame or sorrow into as yet unexplored physical realms, discovering that a woman is stronger in one spot, while another spot demands a different kind of attention, and a third spot is aroused by the various movements of another body. That's how we read each other to the letter, that's how we learned each other by heart, line by line, like the school primer that we read over and over, the same one that other nations had often forced upon us in a translated version, and to which we put up the same resistance as we did to our own environment, one that couldn't fathom the most important thing for both of us was to teach ourselves by ourselves, to get to know our bodies from top to toe, over and over again, to constantly reveal ourselves, to disclose our secrets, which brought us so close together that we couldn't conceive of putting an end to that lust that we shared only with the woods. And not only that. It wasn't just getting wet and getting hard that was important to us. That's why we went beyond the places we reached. That's why it wasn't just our bodies that intertwined like the small leafy climbing plants on the vine. No. Everything that we consisted of we blended together and poured into each other. And I was left completely astonished in the moments when I noticed that she saw the sky as I see it, but the earth differently from me, and how those same and different characteristics carried us along the same river, like two currents measuring their strength against each other, clashing at every moment, since time immemorial—who knows?—perhaps even from the beginning of time, when water first appeared on earth. Thus, what was born from us developed quickly, outgrowing everything that we were both ready and not ready for, leaving no room for us not to have room. And when it gets too tight for you in your own skin and in your own environment, naturally, something must give way. For our parents it gave way to shame, and for our neighbors joy, joy at having found an excuse for hundreds of hours of idle talk, recounting our fate and our misfortune. The goatherd, Trajče, apparently saw us in the woods, me with a bare ass, and Luna with her pert breasts exposed, which, according to the rule, should be strictly reserved for the man chosen by the girl's father, the man who will either take care of them or who will just treat them like cattle bought from a market, depending on the happiness that quite often the girl was unable to choose for herself, but rather was imposed by another. Trajče was apparently disgusted by what he saw. He wasn't quite right in the head, and when he encountered such a sight, he got overly excited and didn't know what to do. The poor wretch felt nauseous and ran off to tell his father, who didn't know what to say to him. Trajče had been in such a blind panic that he forgot about the goats. They got lost in the woods, and it took his father the whole day to round them all up again, after which he had an argument with my father, an argument that all the neighbors had learned of even before it took place, recounting it throughout the whole town faster than a plague, a word hardly strong enough to describe the pain we had to endure after that incident. Then, as often happens throughout history, the words changed their meanings once again. He who loved was a lecherous man, she who loved was a slut. The ugly girls from the town—those who never caught anyone's eye—were saints, and the newly married men who began beating their wives even before their marriage bed went cold—were reportedly good husbands. Then the shade of the beloved tree with which we cloaked ourselves and the softness of the thick grass on which we floated began to resound in the abandoned woods, letting forth such a mighty roar that it split our eardrums—mine and Luna's—and left us deaf to everything and crushed by all.

The Narrator

AT THE TAVERN once again . . .

"Come on now, make it up you two. For Christ's sake, you're neighbors, and here you are fighting over your kids. C'mon, have a shot of firewater and let go of your anger. Come on, order a shot of rakija to clear your throats."

"I don't drink with just anyone. Rakija can turn sour in bad company."

"What d'you mean by that, eh neighbor? Do you want to swallow your drink glass and all, eh?"

"Mitre, keep a lid on it, and stop waving your stick around."

"If I was afraid of your stick, Petse, I would've stayed at home. A dry twig such as that couldn't even wipe the dust off my back!"

"I wouldn't know about that. Just you step on my toes, then we'll see whose back is softer."

"Oh, you weakling. You'd better watch it when you're out hunting, in case there's a bullet with your name on it."

"Don't give me any of your bullet stories, Petse. I can mash your sort up like bread and milk, and lap them up with one hand."

"You lap up quite a bit, I see, but just watch you don't choke on it. This 'bread and milk' here's got bones in it, it's not harmless. My hands aren't this big and strong from spinning yarn. Nor from beating empty straw."

"Petse, if you throw one more jibe at me, neither wife nor kids will be able to recognize you tonight, is that understood?"

"Wife and kids?! Whose wife and kids, dammit . . .?"

"Now now, you angry fighting cocks, smooth those ruffled feathers, dammit. If you want to fight, go outside. Don't give me any headaches. Hmph! You come in here and make a scene after only one glass of rakija!"

"Mandža, you're not throwing me out by any chance, are you?"
"Listen to him now, 'you're not throwing me out.' You're here
every day, how can I throw you out? But you shouldn't fight.
It's wrong. I don't even know why you hate each other so much.
Elsewhere they're clobbering us, they've finished us off, and now
we're coming to blows with one another. Don't be like that. It's
wrong. If you've got a problem, sit down, have a dozen shots of
rakija—not just one—and settle the problem like men, not like
this, raising a hand against each other. Don't do that. It's not
good. It's not right. Here, Father, you tell us whether it's right
or not."

"First, pour me a glass of wine. Some of that black wine.
The thick one that flows like oil, not that sour stuff."

"Here, Father, here. May it turn to blood, if the Lord above
so grants."

"From your mouth to God's ears, my son. Oh, oh, quite so!
Wine is God-given. It's said that it's the blood of Jesus. Is it
right to spill it on the ground? No. And for blood to be spilled
isn't right either. All I can tell you is that fighting is the devil's
right hand, and now he's looking on in exultation, he's rejoicing,
while the angels above weep. Well, you two do what you like.
In the end, you'll find out whether or not St. Peter has barred
the door to you."

"Okay, Father, you've had your say, now pull yourself
together. Go on, drink up and shut up; don't you start waving your stick around as well. Mandža, give us the bill for the
rakija, I don't feel like drinking anymore. A man can't even get
any peace in a tavern. Goddamned good-for-nothings. And fix
the door, Mandža. I can't even open it or shut it. Here, shut it
yourself."

*

"Well, my door's no better'n Mandža's. Ah well, maybe I'll fix it
sometime. In wintertime, when there's not so much work to be

done. Wife, I'm home. Go on, pour us a stiff one. Some of that white stuff, not that amber one."

"Pipe down, not so loud! You can see the kids are asleep."

"I can see that, but you just pour me one or else I'll show you later on."

"I'll pour you one, like I do every night. Have I ever not poured you one? There you go."

"Listen here, that old hick—Luna's father—I can't stand the sight of him anymore. Talk some sense into me or else I'll do something crazy, d'you here? In case the rakija leads me into a situation I don't need to be in and I end up rotting away in some prison because of a louse like him. I don't feel like lying in prison."

"Well then give him half the fields and he might be persuaded by that. What else can I tell you?"

"Holy Shit! Half the goddamned fields. That's easy for you to say. But then where'll we sow our crops? What'll we have to eat in winter? Especially if he doesn't give us anything, that goddamned hick. I don't want to give him anything. Then to become in-laws with him—that goddamned wedding. I'm not dancing an oro with him, have you got that?"

"I've got it, I've got it. But I'm not sure you get it. It's not a matter of who you'll dance an oro with, but who your son'll have your grandkids with."

"You always twist things around. A person can hardly talk to you. Go on, get out of here . . . go do something, do some work . . . go on."

The Narrator

"It's as if everyone hates everyone else in this world. There's so much hatred around, it's enough to scare one into thinking that tomorrow mothers might even begin hating their own children. There's always someone waiting to trip you up, to say something bad about you, to curse you behind your back. It's not for no reason people say—may the neighbor's goat die. Why? To wish them rotten luck, that's why. Because nobody can stand anyone that's better off than them, that's why. And out of sheer spite, those who were decent to begin with don't stay like that because they've been stepped on by others."

Something or other like that Sunny's father once said to him, recounted here in my own words. It was one of those rare moments when his father spoke to him like a father. Actually, Sunny loved his father as much as he hated him.

LUNA'S FATHER WOULD not hear another word about me taking her as my wife. Luna begged her mother, who pleaded with her husband, and he slammed his glass down on the table and told her that as long as he was alive, he'd never give her to me. The matchmaker wasn't permitted to ask for her hand again, that's how things went in these situations. Another way had to be found. Either I elope with her and we end up starving to death, or my father or her father or both of them together murder us, or else I go abroad to work and return with some gold nuggets that would win both our fathers over, that would allow them to mend fences, to repair the invisible cracks in their houses, not unlike the cracks in their souls that either nature had arranged that way or that time had made like that—though which it was, I'm not sure.

During that terrible period, when things were at their worst and I thought that there was just no escape, it seems once again I felt a certain closeness toward my father. One night, he came home as usual, wiped the troubled look off his face—my mother had already filled up his flask—but I wasn't expecting him to say anything I hadn't already heard before, while my grandmother was sitting there fuming over the neighbors who were gossiping about her because of me, and feeling sad because years of wisdom had taught her what it's like when the most cherished person in your life is far away. And who knows, maybe even her own experience had taught her that too? As I was saying, in such a moment, harsh words once more escaped my father's lips, but this time they seemed tempered by gentleness, and we couldn't believe our ears because gentleness almost never entered our house together with my father.

"Wife, pour your son a shot of rakija. And you, you little good-for-nothing, sit down here and listen up. Mitse the pigeon-keeper is going abroad to work. But far away. To America. If we give some money to that peasant for a father your girl has, his eyes'll light up, and that's all he'll need. That's my advice to you. I can tell Mitse to take you along with him, but you do what you want," he said, and, in place of tears, the room filled with joy, which was so out of the ordinary that my grandmother crossed herself repeatedly that night in thanks to God.

And so one morning we got up at the first cock's crow. The low round dining table was laden with food—to remain etched in my memory that way, and to ensure it would be full to overflowing when I returned. My mother placed a jug on the doorstep filled, I imagine, with her own tears and my father told her not to cry or he'd thump her one. Her son had become a man, and that was no reason to cry, but instead reason to be happy. My grandmother threw a handful of wheat over me, filling her hand up with as much of it as she could, believing that a handful of wheat would ensure I wouldn't go hungry over there. I kicked over the jug so that it broke into pieces. It was meant to bring good luck, but one of the pieces struck the dog's eye. Our neighbor muttered quietly to himself that this wasn't a good sign, and then bit his lip when he realized that my father had heard him, but was relieved when, instead of him, my father kicked the dog, and said to it: "Goddamned fucking dog!" To conclude the going abroad ceremony, my mother tipped out a glass of water behind me to ensure that things would flow smoothly for me. And now here I am aboard the ship. Somehow, my mother managed to inform Luna that I would be going away and to wait for me, as only she knows how to wait. Luna told her that if there was hope for us, she would sleep away all the empty months and years with one eye open, so I was able to set off on my journey with an easy heart. And here I am, as I was saying, having woken up with the hope for a better tomorrow on the ship slicing through the waves.

The Narrator

WHEN DIRTY RAINS come that's not to say problems have been born, but rather that they have tumbled down from the cover of darkness. Problems aren't born; they've been around since time immemorial, from the time of the first kiss between two clouds. And they're merely waiting for the right moment to make their appearance, to come out and to bare their teeth. That story has been repeated ever since humans first appeared on earth, and it won't stop, at least no one so far has foretold that it would fade away, that its force would vanish. On the contrary.

Sunny

Mornings in unfamiliar surroundings are always bleak. I gave a start and woke up for the first time aboard the ship. People were going about their morning business noisily. Mitse told me that we were allowed up on deck. I climbed up and the cold sun drenched me, just like the one back home that in winter my grandmother described as angry and fond of pinching cheeks, after which I dreamed of winter as a huge, pale gray, feathery cloud with pudgy hands, delighting in pinching my cheeks, and in a booming voice, as though emanating from a cave, saying, "Oh, oh, oh . . . little cheeks, little cheeks, oh, oh . . . I'll pinch them, I'll make them red." After that dream, I squealed and squirmed like a pig before slaughter when at Easter my grandmother took us outside and rubbed our cheeks with a red-dyed egg, tracing the sign of the cross over our faces with it, starting at the forehead, moving down to the chin, then across each cheek, saying: "red and white, alive and well, red and white, plump with health." That's how it was. That's what I remember of those childish problems, which seem funny to me now, but at the time seemed like the end of the world—which is probably true of all problems, because almost all of them look small to us once they've gone.

But, to cut a long story short, my first meeting here, to my great misfortune, was with a man from Belgrade, from Serbia. The old man, around sixty-five if not a day older, had a problem with his left leg—his main escort being a walking stick—though at the time, I didn't know that he also had a problem with his wife, twice as young as he was, and who was looking for all the things in her husband that the old man didn't have. He got her, he said, from a village. Her parents weren't so much poor as they were greedy for a few extra gold coins, and the fact that afterward their neighbors would recount with envy that their daughter had gone off to the city, that she had swapped a donkey for a horse, and that the owl had transformed into an eagle. He immediately complained to me about his diminished sense of vitality for someone his own age, adding that his initial joy on turning up with that dew-covered rose in Belgrade soon turned to despair because, as he put it, had he even given that deranged woman a palace it would have been far too little and she wouldn't have been satisfied. Turning a blind eye to things, the merchant and his wife went to live in Vienna. But even there the same story awaited him. And so, there was nothing else that could be done about it, the old man said. Both his sons were in America and they sent money for him to join them, where at least they too could keep an eye on the unruly dragon—as the old man referred to her—whom he greatly suspected was also warming other men's beds, not just his own. And he began to tell me things, as though in one breath.

"I see her, goddamn all her kind, we're strolling through Kalemegdan Park, and I see her, goddamn all her kind, staring at others. At both men and women. She was just looking at what they were wearing, she says to me. 'Goddamn you and your kind,' I say to her, 'I'll see to it that your eyes are cast down—down in the dirt, like your mother's, because I'm sending you back to the village where you can scream until you're blue in the face, you ungrateful little snake,' I say to her. And she says to me, 'Honey,' she says, 'don't be so harsh. Darling, you're scaring me, and I won't be able to sleep at night,' she says to me. Goddamn her to eternity. Dammit, but she knows how to get to me, damn that knowing of hers. And I tell you, she'll say something like that to me, and I lose all strength to send her packing. And at night I began to beat her up, to slap her around a bit, but after a while, she grabbed my hands, she grabbed them and I felt weak—goddamn old age as well. Before, I could twist a Turkish spine in my hands like a wet rag, but now it's I who have become a wet rag, goddam old age.

"The women in the neighborhood started coming around and telling me all sorts of things about her. 'Milutin,' says Spasa, 'Milutin, you're such a good man, there's no other man as good you. You and Mira were like one—one made of two. But this

new one, Milutin, she's turned out to be quite the wayward
one. Milutin, may I never speak ill of a soul, may I never say
anything that shouldn't be said. But if she were living with me,
I'd tie her up with a belt, just loose enough so she could reach a
piece of bread,' Spasa says to me. 'Everybody in town is talking
about her; she's the main topic of conversation from what I can
gather,' she says to me. 'They're also talking about what she used
to do when she was living in the village. I'm not sure if you know
anything about that. Milutin, let me ask you something,' she
says to me, 'you know that Mira and I were like sisters . . . let me
ask you then, at night, when you go to bed—how should I put
it—now don't get me wrong, I'm not asking you about something else, God forbid, but when you go to bed at night, do you
sleep soundly? You should check to see if she leaves the house at
night. Now, I don't know, I don't want to say anything bad, but
you should be on your guard,' she says. Meanwhile, I can recall
Spasa as a young girl, who was as fresh as a dewdrop, and I say
to myself: if I had my youth now, I'd be all over you like a rash,
but I don't have the strength, so I'll just sit here and listen to
you babble on—what else can I do? And she says, 'Why all this
talk? Well, you know what people are like—at times they make
a mountain out of a molehill,' she says. 'However, if I were you,
I'd tie her up at night. But then, I shouldn't go on about it, in
case you take me the wrong way,' she says. And then I give her
a good piece of my mind and chase her out. 'Go on, get out of
here,' I say to her, 'goddamn you and your kind,' I say. 'All of you
just watching Milutin with envy because Draga is as beautiful
as Mira was, goddamn all the dead and her too. Why did Mira
have to die so young, goddamn her? Maybe it wasn't because of
the beatings I gave her . . . Her eye used to wander too, but not
as much as this one's, goddamn her.'

"And just as Spasa had said, the next day I come home and
I hear a voice. I see the neighbor, sitting down at the table, acting as though it's his place, goddamn him and his sort, and he's
telling her something. And my wife's spinning the glass around
in her hand, as if she's fondling it, goddamn all her kind. And

then I burst in. 'We're going to Vienna,' I said. No one's going to make an ass out of Milutin in his old age, goddamn 'em.

"Things didn't work out with my sons either. They went off to America, and wouldn't hear a word about coming back. They reckon where we come from life's hard and there's no money; while over there, life's hard but there's money, goddamn them. I created them, I struggled to look after them, for neither one of them to stay behind to look after me, and so now I'm supposed to cross the oceans to go and be with them, throwing up like a seasick little kid at my age," said the old man.

And after telling me his life story in just a few minutes— the way people often do because they've got nothing else to say, preoccupied as they are with their own fate, which they've made no effort to change—she appeared as though out of the blue. Then, once again, my tongue went dry because of a woman, and I lowered my gaze the way I did when I first saw Luna. I greeted her without looking her in the eye, struck by her appearance from which I quickly gathered that for anyone to exert control over her, to tame that liveliness and unpredictability in her nature, two of me would hardly be enough to do the job, let alone someone like the old man. I wasn't merely aroused by her slender figure and her clothes, such as we had rarely seen in those days—a feathered hat with a veil for the sun that she had no need of that morning; she twisted the folds of her open veil in a pronounced way, swinging her hips slowly and imperceptibly, but clearly enough for me to see that those moves weren't her usual ones, that she was performing them with a clear purpose in mind, the way animals always adopt a different pose when they catch sight of their ideal partner, parading, fighting, roaring, and challenging everything around them, just so they can win over what might seemingly make their head explode. As I was saying, I wasn't just aroused by her body, which had generous proportions in the best sense of the word, but also by her eyes, the glow of her piercing eyes that seemed to fear nothing, that didn't avert their gaze from anything, from any challenge, eager to take in more and more, as if they were fleeing the feeling of spent youth.

"Hey you, introduce yourself," the old man said to her, and she held out a white-gloved hand and squeezed mine the way a man does, locking her eyes on me and making me weak at the knees.

"I'm Draga," she said. "What's your name?"

"My name's Sunny," I said, with my gaze fixed firmly on the ground.

"Oh, you're a neighbor. I was born somewhere down there as well, not far from Macedonia, just outside of Vranje," she said with some joy, but also with a strange haughtiness in her voice.

The old man reproached her:

"Come on, don't talk so much. Avert your eyes, goddamn you and your kind," he said to her.

"You're so rude. Invite our neighbor to tea with us," she said to him while looking at me, staring at me like no other woman in my life, with piercing eyes that made my manhood stir and swell. I put my hand in my pocket, took hold of my manhood, and a frenzy seized me. The thought immediately flashed through my mind that for the first time such desire wasn't directed toward Luna; rather, the same thing that drew me toward Luna rose up within me again, only this time kindled by another woman. I'd been completely disarmed. I didn't know what to think or what to do.

And to make things worse, the old man said:

"Finally, a sensible suggestion. Come on neighbor, let's go and have some tea," he said, and we sat down in the ship's canteen.

Even though it wasn't hot, she cooled herself with a fan, a strange object that I also saw for the first time. I stared at the old man, trying not to look at her, although an invisible force was drawing me toward her. Careful Sunny, I said to myself, compose yourself, find somewhere private and release some of the pressure in your loins. And that's exactly what I did. I excused myself and said I'd be back quickly. I went into the restroom from which I emerged a little while later.

When I returned the old man had dozed off. Draga motioned to me to sit down, displaying her gloved hand with a ring on it, but my glance wandered to her bare forearm above the glove. I couldn't wait for the old man to wake up. I mumbled something incomprehensible, turned around—I don't even know in which direction—and went back down below deck, feeling broken and defeated on my own account, on account of my manhood, which I promptly discovered I couldn't control that easily. Little did I realize that in the future it would bring me the sweetest joys, and in turn dissatisfaction that would fill me with disappointment and force me to confront the terrible fact that I'm incapable of remaining faithful in love.

As I was saying, down below deck again, I mulled things over and over in my mind, paying no attention to Mitse telling me about the job he'll get, how he'll fill up with money and return home to buy his children new clothes for Easter, and probably nothing for his wife because he doesn't even mention her. And as for himself, he'll buy the most expensive carrier pigeon and a gold ring for around its foot, so there's somewhere for the messages to be kept, which, truth be told, will never be sent to a living soul. I sat there in the miserable state that arises when, after only a short time, you begin thinking about someone else and not the one for whom you would've moved mountains, the one who's meant the world to you. And I wondered to myself, if you can't remain true to the one most important person in your life, then was she ever that important? I don't know what's wrong with me, I said to myself. But what I do know is that I couldn't be more confused. If God himself had come down to earth and told me that I would think about another woman, I would've slapped his cheek, so to speak, and I would have said to him—with all due respect toward his noble role in this world, as some have understood it to be, while others have made use of it as they shouldn't—I would've said to him that even he doesn't have the right to say something like that, which would never happen even in a dream! But there you have it, after so many years of such self-assurance, a single glance changed me. Dammit, here's what to expect from a man, I said to myself. As I was saying, I said many things to myself, and I told myself that for the moment I don't have the answer to these questions, so I'll wait and see what the evening and what the morning bring, even if the wait left me with an unprecedented sense of unease.

The Narrator

SIN IS THE oldest tenant. It took up residence in humans from prehistoric times, and linked their eyes with desire when appropriate but also when not. No one has ever escaped it. For it is written: a thought can also be sinful. And there is no person in this world who hasn't entertained a sinful thought, and very few who haven't consorted with sin. If any at all . . .

Sunny

AND WHAT DID the morning bring? It brought the same thing, what else could it bring? That same sense of unease descended upon me from my uneasy dream in which, for the first time, Luna appeared to me as a monster. She wanted to take something from my hands. What it was, I didn't see. She opened her mouth and fire leapt out, and at the same time flames shot out from her hair and her eyes, from those places I'd so often gazed at and caressed. I woke up, and my feet immediately took me of their own accord up on deck, although at the same time it was as if they were also dragging me back, damn them for not dragging me back that first time. Neither she nor the old man were up there. For three days I went up onto the main deck where the ship's wealthiest as well as poorest passengers had the rare opportunity to observe each other—from a respectable distance, of course. For three days I saw neither of them, and I felt somewhat relieved after deluding myself that my uncontrollable craving for the Serbian woman's juices was due to seasickness and fatigue. Fine, but, as is often the case, whenever a man begins to feel a little over-confident his wings are clipped. My fragile calm was disrupted on the fourth day when I almost succeeded in remaining below deck, deliberately lying to myself about not wanting or needing to see her again, that slut who felt no disgust at warming the body of an old man, and who probably gave herself to anyone who wished to stray from the straight and narrow. But all the defense mechanisms I came up with weren't enough to prevent that inevitable meeting. They were seated, like a well-to-do couple, on some comfortable deck chairs. The old man was dozing, while she hooked me with her gaze and reeled me to her side, clearly betraying a desire to be crushed by the weight of my presence. I didn't resist, even though the whole time I wondered why I was moving toward her. I told myself repeatedly that this was a terrible mistake, that I had to flee from temptation, but it gradually dawned on me that it wouldn't let me get away until some sort of a miracle occurred. But miracles rarely, if ever, come to pass . . . Quite simply, I surrendered. I gave myself over wholly to the situation, as though being driven in a lavish carriage that was shaking me to the core, and making me wince with fear at every crunch of the pebbles under the wheels.

First Story

What do I say, what can I say? . . . During those days, the old man would go off to bed early, and we'd lie down together later on. Draga would slip out of the old man's bed once he'd fallen asleep, exhausted from the seasickness and from some pills that she put in his water. In those first three days, Draga told me three stories that seemed like three dreams. Were they real or not? I don't know . . . Did I learn anything from them or not about how and why fate had led her to that ship?

I heard the first story as I was walking her back to her cabin. After she told me the story—before she told me that we would see each other the next day—she took hold of the door-knob, and before entering the room stood there for a moment facing the door. I waited for something out of this world to happen; the same as with Luna . . . Draga turned her head around slightly, just enough for me to see the way her eye carefully sought me out, and a new look spilled from her eyeball, seizing me like an unpredictable storm. Then for the first time my gaze didn't fall to the ground as though cast down by her look. Damn it, and damn me too . . . But as I was saying, before this look, as I was walking Draga back to the cabin, to my great surprise, she told me about her first kiss, the one that occurred soon after she started playing the mother in her childhood games with her friends, who played her children that had to obey her; if any of her friends insisted on playing the mother, she rapped their fingers with a stick or argued with them until they left. And she persuaded all the others to tell off that friend as well. That's what she told me with a sweet smile, as though borrowed from another time.

"Do you like me telling you stories? I love stories very much," she said.

"Yes, I do," I said, as though standing before a door to another world, wondering whether or not to enter.

Draga began to recount the path that led her into marriage with an old man instead of with someone her own age. The

49

story horrified me. It made my stomach turn, while my lower region once again began to stir. I felt as if, at the same time, I was playing with both the devil and the angels. I was shaking all over. A cold sweat drenched me as she recalled those events. I will never forget that first story, so intense for a young man from a different time and place. It went as follows:

"One day, when I'd grown up a bit, I was holed up in a barn during a rainstorm with Mirka, the girl who used to vie with me to be the mother whenever we played house with the other children in the street.

"Do you want me to show you something?" said Mirka.

"What?" I asked her.

"But if I show you, you have to swear not to tell anyone."

"I swear I won't tell a soul."

"Swear on your mother."

"I swear on my mother's life."

"No, it has to be someone you love even more. Swear on the man who'll marry you when you grow up."

"I swear on my husband's life, I won't say a thing."

"Fine," she said, and she began to lift up her cloak.

"I have a scar here," she said, pointing just above her private parts. "And here," she said, and she showed me everything, even what shouldn't be shown, and she said: "And here, my skin is patchy. I caught some kind of a disease, and white spots appeared. My skin is turning white in places, and the spots are increasing. No one will have me as their wife when I grow up because, by then, my body could be covered all over in white spots like a cow," she said.

I reached out my hand, I touched the skin near her tender spot, and she screamed as though in terror.

"What are you doing?" she shouted.

I stared at the patch of skin, and told her that if she became spotted all over when she grew up, I'd take her in at my place, and that we'd be sisters, and no one would say a thing, not even my husband.

With her underpants down around her ankles, Mirka hugged me, and something inside me turned over. That's probably when the devil entered me, and I kissed her cheek.

"I will always be your sister," I told her, and I kissed her again. My lips stayed on her cheek, close to her mouth, slightly longer than the previously friendly kiss. Mirka pushed me away, and said:

"Don't kiss me. You're not my husband!"

Since that time, I never felt normal in her company. I wanted to prove to her that she was my best friend and I always stole a chance to kiss her. After a while, she wouldn't let me kiss her goodbye, so I told her that she'd have to let me kiss her once every day, otherwise I'd tell everyone that she had spots down there. What's more, I told her that I had to check her regularly to see if any new spots were appearing, or else I'd immediately tell everyone about the scar. Mirka developed a stutter that never disappeared. She stopped coming out to play so often. A year or two later, when I grew up a bit, I got scared of what I was doing. I withdrew inside myself, and I didn't tell anyone about the spots and the kisses. I prayed every night for the devil to leave me. Every night, for several years. Until Mirka got married. At a very young age. She asked her mother to help her get married in another village. And in fact, she became a bride in another village. When they came to take her, I kissed her for the last time, in her bridal attire," Draga finished the story just before we reached the door of her cabin.

"Why did you tell me all this?" I asked her.

"Because I've never found anyone to whom I could tell it before," she said.

"Are you scared of me?" she asked, after taking hold of the doorknob.

By then I knew that my gaze would not be cast down by her look that seized me like a storm. And I went off to the restroom.

The Narrator

THAT NIGHT, BEFORE he went to sleep, Sunny played with the shadows cast by the paltry light that fell across his bed. He held his hands to the light, while it produced various figures. One of the figures asked the question: where am I? The second asked: what am I doing? The third was terrified. The fourth wanted to get up and venture into the unknown.

THE NEXT MORNING I had just one hopeful thought: that it's not a question of the same level and strength of feeling I had—that I still have—for Luna, but rather something quite different. I knew I shouldn't see Draga again, but I also knew I couldn't not see her. Quite simply, I was divided in two. My soul was crying out, but my mind wasn't listening. An argument with my spiteful mind ensued:

"Just once more tonight. I won't do anything; I'll just see her tonight and never again. If I have to, I'll even tell Luna."

"No, I won't tell her."

"But if I don't tell her, then I'm lying to her."

"No, I'm not lying to her. I'm not doing anything bad."

"Oh, yes I am. I'm doing something terrible."

"But I can't not go. After all, she's never had anyone she could tell her troubles to."

"So what. That's her problem, not mine."

"Fine, then I won't go."

"But I can't not go."

"And why can't I not go?"

"Because I've never wanted anything more in my life than to see her tonight. And because nothing has ever made me feel so alive before . . ."

That's what I thought to myself, terrified by my own answers in which I found no thought that would justify me, that would divert my river of sinful thoughts, provide a new channel for the evil water to escape . . .

The time to think things over flowed by quickly, while the evening came on slower than the old man's gait.

She stood there upright like victory, while I approached her like a little worm.

"I've been mulling over your words all day," I said to her, "that you've never found anyone to talk to. Why me, exactly?"

"I don't know. Perhaps you remind me of someone I once loved," she said boldly, as though born to stir things up where she both should and shouldn't.

"Why did you marry the old man?"

"Because first, my parents married me off to a boy who was sick, just so they could get their hands on my dowry. He died after two years. I wiped up every drop of blood he spat out. He would soil the sheets. All day long I had to clean up his shit and piss. And blood. From the bed I slept in at night. Just before he died, right before he took his last breath, he grabbed me by the hair with his scrawny hands as if to draw me close, to kiss me, and he started coughing, but he held onto my hair with his hand as though he'd gathered some strength, he tightened his grip on me and coughed blood over me, on my face. He writhed on the bed with my hair in his hands . . . At one point, I struck him on the chest with my fist to make him let go of me. He was breathing in and out heavily, then suddenly his grip weakened, he looked me straight in the eyes, and breathed his last sigh. His parents claimed that I didn't want to visit his grave every day, that I was to blame for his death, and that I hadn't looked after him as well as I should have, so they sent me back to my parents. Two or three months after he died, I found out that I was pregnant. My mother took me to some woman in the town. I don't know what she did to me, but she took something out of me. Out of the corner of my eye, I saw something that looked like a lump of flesh, without eyes, without a mouth, without ears. An unformed piece of flesh. I wasn't in my right mind for a long time after that. And no one else wanted to have me," she told me all this in one breath.

My gaze no longer feared meeting hers. Before taking leave of her, she asked me: "Which city are you going to?"

"To New York."

"Us too," she said, and in the gap between her parted lips were inscribed numerous desires, countless desires to make up for her wasted youth.

The Narrator

EVERYTHING IS AS it seems and nothing is as it seems. The truth is one and many.

Third Story

ON THE THIRD night she turned up half drunk. The old man had some rakija in the cabin, and she got tipsy.

"D'you know what? Everything I told you yesterday was made up," she said. "The man who died was my father, and the woman—my mother. She remarried later on. That story about the unborn baby is made up too. Everything's made up."

"Why?" I asked.

"I don't know. I like making things up. I've always enjoyed inventing things, living in imaginary worlds. Even as a child. My mother used to say to me, 'you've never grown up, you've remained a child.' Or things like, 'you've gone crazy.' The truth is that, after Mirka got married, I saw a neighbor playing with himself beneath a tree in the field. You don't mind me telling you these things, do you? I trust you, I don't know why. After all, I'm human too, I want to talk about the things that weigh on me. You can judge me later if you like . . .

"A few days later, I saw that neighbor again. A young man, around my age. I didn't move away. I watched what he was doing as if in a daze. But this time he saw me too. He got startled and fastened his waistband. After that, he spread lies about me all around the village. That I'd watched him as he was taking a piss, that's what he said. My father tied me to a tree, and summoned everyone in the village to come and spit at me. And they spat on me, every last one of them. 'Slut, demon, prostitute,' they called me every name under the sun. Even the children called me names, challenging one another to see who could spit at me from the farthest distance. They began tying me up at home too so I couldn't go out. I was the topic of gossip in the neighboring villages. I didn't have a single friend or anyone to talk to. That's why I had to marry the old man. In Belgrade and Vienna things were different. I began to read various books. Do you know that in America women can go to school? They can even become doctors. I'm going to become a doctor. I found a book about doctors. I carry it with me always. If the old man won't let me study, I'll just run away. It's a big place, no one will ever find me. Will you help me if I need it?"

"I'm going to America to earn the money to win a girl's hand," I said.

Draga's look darkened, only for a moment, and then after that, as if resurrecting the mother from her childhood games, she said sternly:

"You will help me!"

Fourth Encounter

AFTER THAT, EVERYTHING proceeded as in her childhood game. For several nights she led me all over the ship. We strolled and looked around. We explored. We gazed at the stars. We laughed. We did whatever she wanted to do. I was petrified the whole time. Whenever she pulled me by the elbow or whenever she touched me, even by accident, I told her about Luna. Not everything. And some things I even made up. I didn't tell her about the woods; instead, I told her that they wouldn't give Luna to me as my wife because we were poor. I told her that she was the most beautiful girl in the town, and added that, right from the start, even as kids, she had loved only me. Until I began to tell her about the bruise on Luna's eye. When I told her that I said to Luna: "I'm going to beat up your father," and when I mentioned our twin tear, she cut me off, and said:

"Do you want me to tell you something?"

"What?"

"I have a scar," she said. And without waiting for me to say yes or no, in the darkness of the deck, behind the ship's ropes, she pulled down her skirt and showed me her scar, just above her thing down there.

At that moment, Heaven and Earth merged for me. I shrank into myself. My feet gave way and I sat down slowly, like a man intoxicated.

"Touch me," she said.

My hand went there of its own volition. Soft folds of gathered up skin under my fingers.

"I'll give you everything that a woman gives to a man, if only you'll help me," she said.

Words failed me, and my thoughts evaporated, leaving a space for something new, something I wasn't prepared for.

"God will punish us," I said to her, but my gaze remained fixed on her small scar, as hers had dwelt on her friend Mirka's.

"Are you Mirka?" I asked.

"It doesn't matter, even if I am. God has no reason to punish us because once we arrive in America we'll get married," she said to me, standing there with her bare flesh exposed to the moonlight. "Do you know that in former times the concubines slept with the Ottoman bey every night? It's also said that the bey passed on the freer ones to the commanding officers, the viziers, the sentries, the pashas, and the district beys. Maybe even to the captains, the irregulars, the corporals, the lookouts, and the sergeants. Did God punish them? No. They ate Turkish delight and other delicacies their whole lives," she said.

"I'm going to America to earn the money to win a girl's hand," I repeated.

"Then why are you staring at me like that?" she asked. My hand, of its own volition, reached toward her again. I heaved a deep sigh, and experienced a wetness in my pants without having been touched.

"I HAVE A plan," she said on the sixth night. "The old man keeps his money in his underwear. I sewed the pocket for him there myself. I'll steal the money when we're undressing for bed. He'll never find me. America's a huge place. You'll come with me. We'll run away together. We'll live off that money for a whole year."

"Are you crazy?"

"I'm not crazy. I just want to live. What does he need money for? Or me for that matter? Just to show me off. His sons have money. He'll die soon, he won't last forever. Anyway, he'd be better off dead so he doesn't suffer. His mind's almost completely gone. If you want to, we can throw him into the ocean. No one will ever know."

"You're crazy."

"You've already told me that. Think it over tonight. I'll wait for your answer tomorrow. I hope you're not made of weak stuff," she said, and then left.

That night, with one eye I saw what my year in America would be like with Draga, and with the other eye, I saw myself working to earn the money to win Luna's hand.

The Narrator

PEOPLE SAY, THOSE who push their luck pay a price. But they also say: that saying was made up by those who never push their luck and who don't pay any price.

Last Night
Sunny

AFTER THAT NIGHT, we no longer discussed what would happen when we got off the ship. I began to think of Luna less and less. In those few nights before falling asleep, I questioned myself, the way I used to do in childhood: what if I don't return to Luna? Then I repeated to myself several times: I will return, I will return . . .

On the tenth evening we got together quite late. After walking around the entire deck, I led her to the stern, pointing out and naming the stars in the sky, which I never gazed at together with Luna because, with her, we could only escape reality during the day, while with Draga it was only at night.

While we were gazing at the sky, something hard struck me across the head. I fell down in a daze. I tried to get up, and with blurred vision, I saw Draga struggling to wrest the cane from the old man's hands. He pulled, she pulled, he pulled, she pulled, then all of a sudden, Draga grabbed the cane, and threw it awkwardly, and the old man fell to the deck. Then Draga came over and helped me up.

"Get his money," she said to me. I looked at the old man on the ground with a line of blood dripping from his head. I undid his zip. His pants were thoroughly wet. I shoved my hand inside his urine-soaked underwear, as if he'd intentionally pissed all over the money. I took out a bunch of torn notes. There were only two or three good ones left.

"I've torn up and pissed all over your happiness," said the old man, laughing like a crazy man, and coughing up blood. I stood up again, my hands wet with urine. I looked in his eyes that were laughing out of some sort of perverse joy. In them I saw a kind of madness that threatened to erupt in me as well.

"I piss on your brains," I said to him. And I made a move to go back down below deck. Draga ran after me. I shouted at her not to follow or else I'd throw her into the ocean.

"You weakling," she said, "if I ever lay eyes on you again, I'll kill you, you stupid Macedonian." And she went back to the old man.

That night I dreamt another dream. A hearth in someone's house—probably mine and Luna's—flared up and set everything on fire. Just like that. The dream lasted only a short time. I woke up exhausted, but also determined to probe myself to the depths, to get to know myself to the core, so I could return to Luna as a new man. Although she probably wouldn't want someone she didn't recognize; instead, just that familiar young man from the neighboring street near the woods. Then a horrible gnashing sound was heard, as though a sea lion had clamped the ship between its jaws. Everyone got up and we heard those up on deck screaming that the ship was sinking.

The Narrator

DIRTY RAINS COME from afar; they glide effortlessly over a gilded surface, changing its character; they appear as something other than they are, lulling you into the belief that they are your friends, concealing their toothless grins and all the monstrosities housed within them. Everyone has a place for them at home. And there are many who open their doors wide to them.

Sunny

It isn't necessary for me to recount the rest of that story. Nor does it matter for this story how the ship was wrecked; rather just that the chill from the water lodged itself within me, within my soul. Regarding this crucial episode in my life, it's also irrelevant whether or not Draga and the old man survived, or even if perhaps the old man had given me his cane and told me to take Draga to the lifeboat to save myself, at the same time warning me to be careful what I do, because if you allow a snake to go hungry for a few days it will immediately bite you, and its venom could easily contaminate you. It isn't important either how we reached America, or the agony of Golgotha I had to go through, or whether Draga and I kept each other warm with the few blankets on the lifeboats that saved our lives. Nor whether I myself, minus Draga, about whom it no longer matters for this story if she survived or not, was surprised at my own fate in surviving. In those crazy moments, I wondered if everything had happened because of my infidelity, the thought of which rang in my head louder than the gnashing of steel as the ship was being torn apart.

What is important is that now there were two women occupying my thoughts instead of one. And that they began to fight within me. One moaned and whimpered, the other groaned and tugged. As soon as I closed my eyes, both appeared before me. Draga was always the stronger, and displaced Luna. Then I would open my eyes and try once more to only think of Luna, when—pop!—Draga would appear again, uninvited, taking over the whole space. Her sighs eroded time, while Luna's sounded like the whines of a lost kitten. Their breasts were bared, but while Draga's were drenched in full summer light, Luna's were cast in shadow. I closed my eyes tighter but to no avail. One was still sitting cross-legged on a tree branch, while the other sat farther behind her among some dry scrub, like a little cherub . . .

Oh dear me, what path should I take now? I said to myself, and I waited for Luna to return, for a space to open up within me for her alone to lie down in the breast of one who was yearning for her somewhere far away over there . . .

The Narrator

IT IS DIFFICULT to trust anyone in this wide world. How can you when sometimes even those dearest to you, those for whom you've done more than you've done for yourself, know how to hurt you most. Even those you see every day, the ones you share your bed with, even they have it in them to deceive you. And you see them every day. You look them in the eye. And just what is in their souls?

Sunny

I ARRIVED IN America a different person, prematurely aged, and weighed down by a cloud of heaviness that was visible to all. I planned to work for a short while as a day laborer, to not see the light of day—just like back home where in the parched fields day seemed like night—and then to restore my soul to its rightful place, to my homeland where everything is in its place. But rarely do things run smoothly in a person's life. First I met up with Mitse. He'd fallen overboard, upon which he saw himself from high above, as though a part of him had emerged from the icy depths, presumably to stay warm, at which point someone grabbed him and plucked him out of the water, so he was lucky the chill didn't lodge in him forever. Then Mitse and I went off to meet with some of our compatriots, who had even blacker hands than those I wrote about at the beginning. Despite the fact that they were in the Promised Land, their blackened hands showed little signs that they were sipping milk and honey, as we'd been told before we left home. Right away they told us they could help us if we were willing to put our shoulders to the wheel, that with a bit of luck and effort we would be able to go back home with our dreams fulfilled in as little as four or five years, which to me seemed a long time, but to Mitse seemed short. I spat in my hands and said that I would hand over my body to this country here—let it do to my body what it wants, as long as I can return home.

At first I lived with other Macedonians. They called one another 'Brother' because they were compatriots. They didn't mix with Americans, just with each other.

"Where've you been lately, Brother?"; "Fuck all that scrimping and saving, Brother"; "You look burned out, Brother!" That's what they said to each other. And they all behaved as if they'd learned everything in life, while to us newcomers they spoke as though we were greenhorns: we knew nothing and they knew everything. And this is what they said to us all the time: "Well now, just you wait, you don't know anything, you haven't

seen anything yet." That's how Bogdan greeted us. A relative
of Mitse's. Whose nickname was "Woozy." The minute he sat
down at the table, he drained a bottle of whiskey, bemoaning
the fact that the rakija Mitse had brought him, sent over by his
(Woozy's) wife, had fallen into the sea.

"Maybe it's for the best. The missus might've put something in the bottle and we would've all been poisoned like mice,
ha, ha, ha," he laughed like someone who wasn't right in his
mind. After taking a longer gulp, he started talking and didn't
stop until just before going to bed. Mitse listened to him with a
half-opened mouth. I thought his jaw would drop to the ground
from excitement.

"Kid—just wait till you get a load of all the lookers around
here! Listen, there are women here, a whole bunch of 'em, and
they can be had for money. D'you get my drift? In one of those
kinds of places, d'you follow? You're too young, you don't understand anything. And listen, over here it's not like it is where we're
from. Here you can see them naked. Holy Mother of God, I'm
tellin' you Sunny, listen to me, you're teeth are gonna rattle. Listen, you're young; you haven't seen anything, but let me tell you,
don't be scared of 'em. You're giving 'em money, goddamn 'em,
and that's that, d'you follow? And if you can't get it up—you
follow me?—and if you can't get it up, just tell her and she'll get
it up for you. They're hot to trot, they know everything. Hell,
they're specialists, goddamn 'em, hee, hee, hee," Woozy said to us.

"Hey Woozy, go on, tell him why we call you that. Tell
him you great oaf, so we can have a bit of a laugh," they said to him.

"Oh, blast the lot of you! That's all you lot ever want to
hear, may your ears get clogged from hearing it so often. Okay
then, listen up, it was like this: when I arrived here for the first
time—oh my Lord! They took me over to that place, I was about
your age, maybe even younger, and now—listen, listen good—
and when I saw her, I went woozy and immediately passed out,
hee, hee, hee. In a flash. Now, if you black out, don't worry. Take
me for instance, I'm like a mountain. No one at work can outdo
me, goddamn their lazy asses, you follow me?" said Bogdan, and

he didn't stop talking. He was like an old granny at her stoop. He just droned on about his "heroics," but I never heard him say anything good about back home, how or what it was like . . . or at the very least take out a photograph of his kids to stare at sometimes at night before going to bed . . .

At any rate, as early as on the second night, he took Mitse to that place. With borrowed money. Mitse didn't pass out, but when he got back, he appeared somewhat dazed; a frightened smile hung around his lips the whole time, as if the woman there had taken his soul.

"So, you've dipped your wick into an American, hey Mitse, you horny beast. Now you know what it's like over here in America, not like it is back home; that's not life over there, it's misery. You'll see how you'll end up. And this friend of yours here who doesn't say much. You'll see how you both end up staying here ten or fifteen years," the others said to Mitse, who appeared even more pleased.

I never went to any of those places. Ever. But that's why I began to go to bars. Not much at first, but, I told myself that, just like a car's transmission, the body needs oiling at times otherwise it starts to screech and can break down. So, with the other Macedonians we went to places where they served liquor that looked like piss, unworthy of our rakija back home, which isn't artificially colored but gains its golden hue and develops its strength aged in oak barrels that lie in cellars fastened with iron hoops to hold them steady. There, once again, I experienced a shock, as I did every day in that new environment for me where you could never tell who was eating, who was drinking, or who was paying. The women passed by, saying things in an incomprehensible language, and in each of them I saw Draga . . .

Woozy just kept on repeating:

"Oh, my Lord! Take a look at this one. D'you see now? I'm telling you, over here everything's different. D'you see, d'you see?" Woozy remarked, staring pop-eyed.

Apart from those occasional outings to the bars, I didn't mix much with others. And when I wasn't working, I mostly slept or strolled through the town, marveling at the bustling crowds, being buffeted by the multitude of sounds that were as plentiful as the silence we had back home—for me the loveliest sound at that time. A couple of months went by like that. Then half a year, which seemed to me spread out to infinity, contained in the letters that I wrote to Luna, trying to erase Draga who got mixed up in the lines, rearranging them, scattering them, giving them a different hue, damn her and me too . . . In the letters, I didn't tell Luna anything about Draga or the ship or the ordeals that took me far away from her, knowing she lies huddled in bed every night, grabbing hold of a corner of the blanket with both hands, holding it between her hands with her long, bony fingers, clutching it to her breast, and transferring that clutch to her heart. And staring into the dark distance, together with that cursed but familiar feeling of happiness tinged with sadness, because of the thought that she has me forever (ah, poor Luna . . .) but she doesn't—neither then nor in the countless future revolutions of the sun and the moon. Luna, I was sure, read my letters at the same time I wrote them. And when she received them, they became a part of her, and her face grew less troubled as it does for all those who wait. That was my small consolation, which helped me slowly reconcile myself to my fate, to absolve me somewhat of my wrongdoing, which tripped me up as though across level ground. In that half year, in that period too short even for a corn seed to make its way from a shoot into becoming bread, I gradually began to understand and speak the language. I quickly learned many other things about my job as well. The bosses said I was a skilled young man and that I would go far, the same way my mother used to say I was faster than rushing water and sharper than a hoe. While I was learning the language, I was exposed to many new things. And in that way, by leaving myself open to new experiences—in contrast to Mitse who claimed the whole time he felt like crying because he wanted to drink homebrewed rakija and that he dreamed constantly of his warm bed at home, but whose mind was actually on whiskey and cheap women—gradually I began to sense a change in myself, which, naturally, I didn't oppose, even though I wasn't sure where it would lead me. With such a feeling of openness, my visits to the bars, where the women's winks spoke a universal language, became more frequent. Then the words of my grandmother, who used to say that time is the best healer, proved true, like everything that wise woman said. And whole days would go by without my thinking of Draga.

It was here that I encountered my new love, so to speak. Not a woman. And what I still consider more perfect than anything else, if one can say such a thing. It came on slowly, gradually setting my body to shaking, introducing it to new rhythms and pleasures. And if I listened to it completely, it evoked almost the same feeling as when Luna, washing clothes at the river, would partially expose her breast to me, while I, carefully hidden, looked on from afar. I never could tell if she knew I was staring at her and deliberately invited me to look, or if it was just plain coincidence, which I later learned it wasn't. The palpitations that Luna gave me (and Draga too, it's true . . .) I also experienced over here—naturally, of a different kind and from a different source. My new love appeared to me first through the tapping of my foot, at precise moments and at ordered intervals. That love was unfathomable to Mitse, whose mind was steadily being eroded by whiskey, while the women were diminishing the earnings on which his hungry children somewhere far away over there depended. "She," my harmlessly dangerous incorporeal mistress, who in the truest sense can bewitch those with even the tiniest interest in the flurry of individual notes and tones, in taking in from afar the beguiling cacophony of sounds, and in giving oneself over to her completely, was—music! Yes, I was pleased that I hadn't immediately gone in pursuit of new flesh, and yet had found a joy that got me through that hopeless situation. Until that time, I had only ever seen and heard the elders play at weddings in the town center, their knees bent low, sitting atop drums as wedding handkerchiefs twirled in the air, the sound of the zurlas whistling through their mustaches yellowed from bad tobacco as they played Teškoto, that sacred dance of ours, which even shakes the heavens, piercing through the mountain peaks. As did the bellowing of our compatriots, who brayed like donkeys when we all got drunk at night.

But this was something entirely new. New music of the time, which shook my body and gave me a new freedom of understanding. I, Sunny, the ill-fated one, had the luck—or the misfortune—to come to America in the time that succeeded ragtime music, ten years since Jazz had first made its appearance in 1913, when the music of the blues took hold of me and carried me off, carrying me the way a brother carries his own brother across a river without getting him wet, without getting his feet wet. But the music also drove me like the wind that always rips the crown off the linden tree in late fall, and spins it like a top, putting it down safely on the ground in its new and this time eternal resting place.

The Narrator

Back at the tavern once again . . .

"So, Mitre, I hear you've been tellin' people your son's gone off to America to bring back the money for my daughter's hand, eh? Just so you know, I'd sooner flush that money down the toilet than hand my daughter over to your lot. Did you get that?"

"Mandža, tell this guy to stop flappin' his gums or else I'll slug him."

"Petse, come on now, stop yelling. All you ever do when you come here is fight."

"Mitre, look at me when I'm talking to you."

"Mandža, tell this guy to stop bellyaching."

"Petse, come on now, stop all this yellin', for cryin' out loud. Go home and yell at each other. Do I come over to your place to yell?"

"Mitre, it seems you don't know who you're messin' with. Don't give me any of that 'Mandža, tell him this, Mandža tell him that.' If you're a real man then get up and prove it. Let me have it."

"Mandža . . ."

"What's with this 'Mandža, Mandža' all the time? You're always putting Mandža in the middle. Go on then, have it out if you want to, fuck that endless 'Mandža, Mandža.' Well, is Mandža to blame? May your own houses fall down around your ears, you goddamned peasants."

"Well it ain't as if you're some city sophisticate, Mandža. You're a goddamn hick yourself. I'm just askin' you for one more rakija, and to get rid of this fly over here that's buzzing around my head. I'm not sayin' anything else. Go on, bring us one before I take you on as well."

"Mitre, you're wimping out mate, you're afraid to turn around, you son of a bitch. Well, you just sit there; sit there, and let me see how long you stay there."

"Will you folks just quit all that goddamned nonsense. My, my, how this almighty brute speaks. It's as if we've become a pack of wolves at each other's throats. Mitre, don't get up, listen to me, stay in your seat."

"Don't you worry, Mandža. I won't wreck the place. Go on, give us some rakija. I can even sit with the flies."

"You can, but let's see for how long. I'll come looking for you one of these days. And you too, Mandža, I'll have it out with you as well one day, just so you know.

"And fix your door. You can't even open or shut it. Here, shut it yourself."

*

"Dammit, mine's no better 'n Mandža's. Fucking door! Luna, hey Luna, are you there?"

"Yes, father."

"I'll fucking murder you, I will! I've become the laughing stock of the whole town because of you. Pour me some rakija, goddamn you."

"Yes, father . . ."

"I'll marry you off somewhere far away, I tell you. I'll hand you over to some miserable wretch so your back'll break from working in the fields, I tell you."

"Yes, father . . ."

"And stop saying, 'Yes, father.' Go on, out of my sight, you bad seed. And stop your sniveling before I thump you one. Have you ever seen your mother cry? Do you think it's any easier for her? Eh? Go on, get over in that corner and stop your sniveling. No, wait! Tonight you'll sleep outside in the barn. Go on, get lost. Get out of my sight."

"Yes, father . . ."

The Narrator

THE SEASONS ARE already ebbing and waning. New forces of nature are coming to light. At that time, Sunny had no idea, no inkling that his new views were sowing the seeds of the future between him and Luna, the girl who carries the power within to see even that which can't be seen, but who will never see the tear of the queen bee; and not because she doesn't possess the ability to do so, but because Sunny won't lend her a hand.

Sunny

THAT FIRST YEAR I spent drifting between hard work and smoky, laughter-filled bars. I did it with a passion that would be equivalent to the Last Judgement for the people where I came from. I went to take in and experience my newfound joy; and I tried to stay immune to the women who looked at me with different eyes. And those I looked at with different eyes . . . But, about that, all in good time . . .

After a year and a half, I began to keep company with a philosopher, who was around forty years old, and who'd come here from Germany long ago. He approached me while I was sitting on a barstool, and said:

"I have two bottles of wine here: one for me, the other for the saddest man in the world. Would that be you, by any chance?"

I wasn't startled by him. I'd already seen that America was filled with all manner of riffraff—as my grandmother would've put it—and I'd learned to avoid them. But the philosopher's offer was different to all those I'd received up to then, and he shot me a sweet smile; besides which, he looked harmless enough, so I replied:

"I don't know, but what I do know is that I could easily drain that whole bottle."

The philosopher smiled, and said:

"Let's see who does it first."

We raised the bottles to our lips, and watched to see how far down each other got. The wine tasted sour, but I drank and drank, not wanting to give up. In the end, with tears in our eyes from the effort, we both quit before reaching the bottom.

"Goddamn bunch of machos," I said to him in Macedonian.

"What?" he said in English, and we started laughing aloud.

So that's how my association began with the philosopher with whom we didn't swap our life stories at our first few encounters, the way many others do when they first meet, like the old man from Belgrade. The philosopher was a smart and handsome man. He spoke broken English, like me. In fact, he didn't talk much, but he knew the secret of words and truth. I don't know why he kept company with me, but he was practically the only one who never asked anything of me. Instead, he gave me things. By observing him, I discovered that the right way to receive is to give. Without him teaching me, I learned many things from him. And we learned things together. We were caught up by the magic of jazz, of the blues; we savored the black voices, and together in loud drunken voices, we sang "I Ain't Got Nobody, and Nobody Cares For Me" along the streets of New York, laughing and singing: "That's why I'm sad and lonely / Won't somebody come and take a chance with me? . . ." That's how we merged our states of melancholy and desire. I called him brate—brother in Macedonian, and he called me mein Bruder in German, after earlier on, blind drunk, I told him I'd give my right arm for him, and he said he'd give his other arm for me.

So that you have a better understanding of him—or to confuse you even more—it might actually be best to read some of his observations. The ones I read one night when he fell asleep dead drunk, but about which I didn't understand a thing. And which, in the morning, on seeing that I'd fallen asleep with them, he offered to me as a gift, saying: "Read them sometime in the future, to recall the fool you once kept company with in the past." And some of those observations go something like this:

THE PSYCHOLOGY OF TEARS

"It was Anaximander who taught us long ago that our primeval origins are infinite and boundless, and that everything is in constant flux caused by opposites. Had he known that his ontology now applies to psychology and anthropology, and that his theory of 'constant flux caused by opposites' can also be applied to love, he would have then gone to his beloved, and together they would have searched for the meaning of life." This was one of those profound anecdotes the middle-aged philosophy students liked to tell one another, sometime in the early 1920s in America.

"O wise and all-knowing teacher, are all virtues compatible with each other? Such as love and moderation?" the veteran teacher was asked by a curious student, after reading Plato in the room of a building that looked like a place of worship.

"There are no right answers, only right questions," said the teacher.

"Is selfishness the ultimate infidelity?" the student asked.

"Yes." The affirmative answer hardly satisfied the student, because answers should include explanations, and this teacher was apparently too lazy to expound the details.

"The most romantic story in antiquity is that of the love between two men: Alcibiades, the handsomest man in Athens, and Socrates, the ugliest—but also the wisest. Plato tells us that Socrates didn't give himself immediately to Alcibiades, whom he passionately desired, because he wanted to explain to him that physical love is of a lower order, and that love of knowledge, of truth is on the highest plane. Alcibiades then began to desire him even more, and Socrates cried out: 'Eureka! One thing I know—the more you say no to others, the more they want you!'"

That's what the philosopher's observations were like, among which were also several funny ones, like one about a court jester. It went something like this:

"The great king sat alone for weeks. He sat alone in his room for so long that it began to appear to him as both bigger and smaller than his whole life. The king's knights and his supporters became worried, as did the court jester, who grew so worried that he developed a wart on his lip. The knights thought to themselves—our kingdom will collapse, what will we do then? The supporters feared the day would come when they would be replaced by others. The wart began to bother the court jester as he thought it made him look ugly. The great king sat alone in his room for weeks. He sat alone in his room for so long that it began to appear to him as both bigger and smaller than his whole life, is written somewhere, by a teacher or some sage or someone."

"Where did this wart come from? I can't help the king," the court jester thought to himself.

"The court jester woke up one day to find that all those around him were court jesters! He ran out onto the street, and it was the same there! He thought to himself: Marx was right; in the end, we're all the same, and I don't see any that are more identical than others! He ran off to tell the great king that the whole time he had wanted to spit a huge green gob in his face! That all the antics he had performed for him were wrapped in a cloak of hatred, and that he had always coughed, not because he was sickly, but from a strong desire to spit at him. But he was scared he might actually do it, so he swallowed his saliva beforehand. That's the reason he coughed, and not because he was sickly! And now he'll beat him with a stick, not just a dozen times—the way the great king had ordered he be beaten because he coughed in his presence—but a hundred, a thousand times with a stick covered with saliva! And just as he was about to hit the great king, the court jester woke up, coughing up phlegm . . ."

"When he was small, the court jester had a mother and a brother. One day he asked his mother: 'Mom, why did you give the bigger piece of fish to my brother?'"

There, that's what the philosopher was like, like no one else. He was even strange with women. Often, he would win them over, and then just toss them aside. To my question "why?" he replied:

"All in good time. We'll talk about that as well."

And that time came quickly, after I learned the language a bit better. Then we started to really talk. To talk a lot. And along with the desire to share experiences with another, my eyes sought out women's bodies more and more often. Much more often. I wanted to pursue them as much as I didn't want to pursue them. I didn't want it to happen as much as I did want it to happen . . .

The Narrator

LIFE AND TOIL are like that, you can't quantify them; or fathom how big they are with a ruler, or place them on scales to get a sense of how much they weigh. It's the same as for truth.

"Do you know what?"

"What?"

"I can't stop thinking about other women. I want to think only of Luna. Please help me."

"I can't help you."

"Why not?"

"I've told you why. Because I don't believe in love."

The Narrator

THE PHILOSOPHER THEN told a part of his life story to Sunny, a story that could easily have been his own, but which Sunny only half understood . . . It goes something like this, told in his own words, here retold in mine:

"I believe in necessity, in closeness, in routine, but not in love, because I've had everything I've ever wanted and then it all just vanished, blown away like dust in a breeze. And all because of me, not because of them . . . I had many loves. Some I tired of quickly, others just tossed me aside like a piece of moldy meat. Those who tossed me aside were from in my early youth. I talked to them about love, about poetry, about philosophy. I spoke to them as though I were standing before the gates of Heaven, in a frenzy of rapture! They just stared at me blankly, not understanding me. And those who did understand me found me dull. I wondered what the problem was. After all, I'm a good person, I don't hurt them, I read them poetry, I'm smart . . .

"'You're like all philosophers: you read poetry and philosophy, but you don't know anything about women,' a middle-aged prostitute once said to me. After what she said, I naturally began to visit her even more often, and I paid not just for her body, but also for her to talk.

"'Women aren't interested in some daydreamer who lives on another plain, but rather someone who'll protect them, who knows how to listen, and, above all, someone they can show off to their friends. Only then can you recite poetry and discuss philosophy,' said the prostitute, giving me the most practical philosophy or truth or whatever you wish to call it.

"So, at the age of twenty-five, I bought myself a new suit, a top hat and a modern cane, a shiny snuff box, and everything turned around for me. Then I left for America. Here, in ten years my view of the world has been turned upside down, and I don't know where I am, and, to be honest, I don't care anymore where I am or what I'm doing—"

"Why don't you believe in love?" Sunny cut him off.

"Be patient. They say that patience is the mother of all wisdom. I say it's the mother of all those who never got anywhere in life," the philosopher said to Sunny, laughing to himself.

And he continued:

"After the prostitute, I would only recite poetry to the women if they asked me to. But even then with feigned self-importance, telling them that I couldn't do it justice, after which I would read out a powerful verse, just a few select lines to take their breath away, not all of it as I did in the past; they then secretly dreamed of me at night.

"Well, after that . . . after that they began to annoy me. As though the same old story began again. Quite simply, I'd know them by the way they breathed, I'd sense their need to look at me even before they looked at me, I'd anticipate their thirst even before they were thirsty. Their eyes, which looked upon even the blades of grass lovingly, no longer awakened the same tenderness in me; their moist lips no longer had the savor of unexplored delights; their features no longer held any charm; their long feminine fingers weren't new to me; and neither was she, the one I had worshipped as if before an ancient secret, as if before Mother Nature herself, as if before a solitary tree in the middle of the desert. Nor did I have the same thrill from the touch of naked skin early in the morning, when dreams merge with reality, when they take on that unique and unparalleled ability to magnify the beauty of reality as at no other part of the day. True, I never tired of their hips. Never. But that's all that remained, and that's not a true accomplishment. That's what Plato taught us, and you can't not trust him. It bothered me—it still bothers me—because, without exception, even in the most perfect union of two bodies and souls, there comes a time of insincerity. Plato teaches us that love of knowledge is the highest possible aim. And love of knowledge is love of truth, that's how I interpret Plato's meaning. The truth that I could never attain with a woman. I could never tell them everything I feel. I couldn't tell them that I no longer desire them as on the first

day; that often I feign interest while in reality I'm quite indifferent to them; that I desire their friends . . . And not just me,
but, what if it's true that they feel the same way too? That they're
also feigning interest. That they have hundreds of things they
couldn't tell me, the same way that I wasn't able to tell them.
And that they desire others too. Probably even in those moments
when that feeling of togetherness is stronger than everything.

"Well, take you and Luna, for example. You'll never tell
her anything about what you did over here. What kind of love
is that, my dear Sunny? True love? Of course not. And yet you
want to go back to her. Why? To have what you once had?
Love, my brother, exists only in the waning of the moon, in
the small shadow that it casts over us. And when you meet
another woman, it will be the same then too. You will both
experience everything that has to be experienced, and you will
come to the same conclusion. Everything in this world is just
an idea, as Plato said. Nothing is real. In the end, we never see
things in their true light. It's impossible to love like in stories,
my dear Sunny. Although it is possible to live quite happily,
unless you sully your life unnecessarily, like me. Many great
loves have functioned that way. No, not functioned—that's the
wrong word; rather, they floated, flowed and foamed, fluttered
and flew, with sweat, with tears, and with smiles. They guarded
what united their souls, although it no longer existed as such.
But that's something that I just don't understand. That's my
misfortune. I'm not cut out to function like that, even though
many have been happy that way, in their perfect imperfection. I
think that only God can love unconditionally, but I don't believe
in him . . . You may have a different fate, Sunny. You might discover that I was mistaken in my interpretation of Plato or find
a true interpretation of truth and love. You may find another
path that will show you that in this world love doesn't have to
be the same all the time, because, in essence, nothing stays the
same for the simple reason that we change too. Because people
change, things change too—according to my understanding of
Heraclitus. But then again, on the other hand, I change, yet the

same problems always confront me . . . I have no answer, my dear Sunny, none . . ."

"In the beginning, did you think that you'd be with them to the end of your life?" Sunny asked the philosopher.

The philosopher began another monologue.

"At first yes, without exception. For example, with the Polish girl, Magda. My first wife. She was so beautiful, the tenderest girl in the world. I don't know if it was her skin or her voice or her soul that was so tender. Or maybe what appealed was just her father's money, which I squandered in the first year," the philosopher said, laughing like a crazy man again, after which he went on.

"Whenever she walked past anyone, she attracted looks like an innocent story. Her voice, her words I experienced the way a baby experiences its mother's breathing, lying on her breast after crying with hunger. And all that I loved most, I soon began to hate. After a year of tenderness, I began to experience it as something rather soppy. Her need for constant security—which I have to say I enjoyed very much, feeling like the only man— began to bug me. I thought she would attach herself to me and absorb me within her, into her needs. One day I was stroking her hair while she purred like a little kitten, snuggled beneath the covers, pleased that her man was beside her, and that he was the one who made all the decisions, who did all the worrying, who did everything necessary for her to be safe from all harm. And that day I said to myself: So I'm playing the role of the father, not the husband! It sickened me. I got up, I pushed her away, and she probably cried for ages. She may still be crying . . . I left that city. I disappeared."

"Just like that?" Sunny asked in disbelief.

"Yes, just like that," the philosopher replied.

"Didn't you feel bad for her? What did you feel?"

"Nothing. I just wondered if I was selfish."

"And?"

"I both am and am not," said the philosopher, and he began to recount the story of his second love.

"The second one, my dear Sunny, was the complete opposite. A real live wire. She drove me crazy with her passion, her
desire for life, for new experiences. She ventured into unexplored
territory with a fervor that left me speechless. But then again,
she did satisfy me. Or maybe I was also scared because I couldn't
keep up with her. She was a woman with two faces. One smiling, the other sad. And nothing in between. I couldn't keep up
with her energy, while sorrow dragged me down with her. She
was so powerful that I began acting according to her needs. She
wanted me to tell her every day that I loved her, that I would love
her forever. At first, I told her that I loved her before she even
thought to ask me. Then the time came when I said it and meant
it. And in the moment when she realized that something in my
voice had changed, that it wasn't my voice, she told me that she
wanted us to get married. I told her I was leaving . . . Many of
my friends have gone through similar things. But they don't
seem to mind. Maybe some of them don't mind because they
have children, I don't know . . . In the end, my last love got very
sick. She was afflicted by an ailment that transformed her face.
It began tearing her apart inside and out. It even changed her
character. And just when she needed me most, I left. I couldn't
watch her deteriorate. It disgusted me. Quite simply, my love
wasn't aimed at a sick woman, at her ravaged face, but at the
beautiful woman she had once been before she fell ill. I didn't
think twice about leaving her. I knew doing that was just as bad
as when a mother leaves her own child, but, when I looked deep
inside myself, everything within me was saying that, apart from
the disgust I would feel as she worsened, I don't feel anything
else for her. And I left. Like the worst man on earth . . .

"I don't believe in love, because whenever I've had it, it has
always vanished from me and brought unhappiness to those
around me. True, I should believe in love because at first I had
it, which means that it does exist. But I don't believe in its con-
stancy, because it just doesn't have it. And without it, then there's
no love too. At least for me . . .

"That's why the only advice I can give you, Sunny, is
either don't do anything you shouldn't do or do everything you

shouldn't do. But I can see that you no longer need what you once needed, that deep down you don't need it. And someone like that can't go back home, because you will only bring back heartache.

"The answers to everything that happens in a person's life are found after the thing has happened. Even at their wisest, even when they can predict all possible moves, a person can't predict how they'll react to them, because they're no longer the same person they were a year or two ago, as Heraclitus said. The same goes for you. You can't remain true to your desires and to your love, because she's from a different time when you were a different you. At this time and in this place you aren't him, but rather you, and it will always be like that. Yesterday and tomorrow are like day and night. You can't see at night with daylight eyes. You can only find things by touch, enough to know that it's you feeling them, and not someone else. I can't tell you what to do. I can't advise you, because the only true path is the one that will make you happy, and at the same time others too. But often that just isn't possible. If you choose the path of the past, you will choose not to seek your own happiness, which is also wrong; just as it's wrong not to choose the path of the past, which, sometimes—in rare cases—may be the present. Think it over and make a decision, Sunny, even though you've already decided but you still don't want to accept it," the philosopher ended his monologue, and took a big gulp of his drink.

Sunny leaned back in his stool, and a dark gale wafted over his thoughts as though a dirty rain was coming from afar.

The Narrator

IT IS WRITTEN that in other times, more distant than the first words spoken, when love walked the earth, and tears were unborn, man and woman were united in one body. They were sufficient unto each other, locked in an eternal embrace.

Then, because they were one made of two, they became so strong that they intimidated the mighty gods. The gods grew fearful of their divine unity and split the bodies in two. Each poor half immediately forgot the name for food, for water, for the sun, because nothing else mattered to them besides the search for their lost half to make them whole again, everywhere and forever more; and if they did not find their perfect half, if they had not caught scent of the half that made them whole, they died with a tear in their eyes, which was given the name "crying." Since then, from those ancient times, lovers have been searching for their perfect half, and when they find it they become one. However, even when that happens, some other gods separate them again.

SUNNY, POOR THING, was in a muddle. He never put Luna out of his mind, while Draga's scent grew weaker and weaker. But what did it matter when he couldn't resist the temptation of female flesh. He eyed all the women surreptitiously. One particular game appealed to him. The game the philosopher played with women, and which pleased him even more than the union of two bodies. He began to play that game too. He began winning women over, then tossing them aside at the first sign of interest. And after a while, he probably began to understand the philosopher, whom he'd never quite fully understood, perhaps because there didn't seem to be any logic to the philosopher's reactions . . .

At any rate, from then on Sunny's power to seduce women flowed ever more freely. As though he had always possessed it. He didn't say much to them. He would just unexpectedly brush aside an unruly lock of hair from their cheek, running the tips of his fingers from their ear down to their neck and to their naked shoulders, staring openly into their eyes; the women knew then that he was staring into their bristling souls and at their lowered gazes.

After taking leave of them, they would go to bed with the thought that they would see him again the next day, and that they would stay in his mind. But the following day he wore a different face. He would respond flatly to their questions until they felt as if they were uninteresting, and began talking about everything and anything, just to break the uncomfortable silence that Sunny had created. After that he would say that he was going out for a drink, and end up with some other woman; or he would simply just leave.

That's how he toyed with women, but he wouldn't sleep with them. He needed female flesh but he was saving himself for Luna, at least that's what he said. Sunny knew quite well that such a lie could not even fool a child; that he was just deluding himself, that there was nothing more worthwhile in this world, but that's the only concession he allowed himself. To lead them on, to feel as strong as a mountain, and then to fling them off. And at night he would torment himself with his mixed up thoughts, crowded with female bodies and distant Luna.

Long before that, his mind and body had already accepted the fact that he could never again think only of one woman. But also that he would never stop being haunted by their apparitions, which would always get the better of him. He knew that already, the way the grass remembers the bear's tread, the way the chicken is aware that it's missing one of its eggs, the way the tree is overjoyed at autumn's golden hue, even though it knows that it's slowly beginning to shed its leaves.

But that wasn't the greatest danger. She appeared as though in a vision, as though a dirty rain had brought her, after Sunny had become fully aware that not only could he not think of just one woman, but also that as soon as one smiled at him—one who can tell the difference between the salt of a fake tear and that of a real tear, and one who's also learned from experience that there are only a few times in life when the corners of one's mouth truly tremble in the presence of another—well, it was then he learned that he would never be at peace. And at the same time he must sink deeper. There was no other way. That's when he met Marianne.

The Narrator

WHEN SHE WAS a young girl, Marianne saw a bird flying joyfully over a field, flitting from tree to tree; its song was so lovely that even the sun's rays changed their direction on hearing it. Every day, from afar, so as not to frighten it, she listened to the bird's song decked in bright colors. Until one day she stood beneath the tree with the bird's nest. And she saw that the bird was flying from tree to tree merely to catch insects.

Marianne

WHEN I WAS a young girl, I saw a bird flying joyfully over a field, flitting from tree to tree; the bird sang so sweetly that I was sure it was summoning its true love. Every day, from afar, so as not to frighten it, I watched the bird, and listened to its song. Until one day I stood beneath the tree with the bird's nest. And I saw that the bird was flying from tree to tree merely to catch insects . . . That marked the beginning of the end of my childhood in France. After that, all my childish fantasies shook within me and shattered like glass. Everything went by as though shrouded in a fog . . . Several times I, too, flew from tree to tree, but happiness never came to me. Not even with the philosopher here in America. When I first saw him, he immediately looked familiar to me, as if I had known him in another place and in another, happier time. Although, as my father used to say, all times are happy and unhappy; it just depends on how you see them and what you make of them. I never agreed with my father, who spoke wisely, but almost everything he said was a truth for which we had no use. Not only was it of no use, it was also a hindrance to us, because he was one of those people who thought knowledge of the truth would bring him much. And while we waited for him to bring us something, he brought us nothing. And so we waited the whole time, us more than him because he was as full of hope as we were lacking in it.

The philosopher was leaning on the counter with his powerful arms. And he knew all the truth that my father only thought he knew. Not only that, he had everything he needed to have—a body sculpted like marble, in other words, sculpted like a god. Because of him, I began reading poetry again, and studying philosophy. It had become fashionable to read and study, modern and wonderful.

He was always in strange company, but with beautiful women. He never even glanced at me . . . Until one day he came and asked me:

"I have two glasses of wine: one for me, the other for the saddest woman in the world. Would that be you, by any chance?"

My throat clenched, and—berating myself later on that night, when I went over all the words we had said to one another, wondering why I had said what I said—I replied:

"What do you mean, 'the saddest'? What are you implying by that?" my words rushed out.

"Then this glass isn't for you. Fine. Goodbye then, beautiful French girl."

"But no, I would like some wine," I said to him.

"Tomorrow perhaps," he said, and turned to go. However, he stopped, turned around again, and handed me the glass.

"On second thought," he said, "I will tell you the story of the Titans from Plato. Have you heard it? It's a myth in which Plato recounts the story of the Titans, how originally they were male and female united in one body, and then after that the jealous gods split them in two," he said, and he began recounting the myth, leaving immediately after he finished telling me the story as though he hadn't been here at all . . .

And he did that all the time. For months. I saw him do it to other women too. He would dazzle them, win them over, and then just abandon them. As though none were worthy of him. So I wondered, I pondered, I justified him to myself, and said, well maybe he had the perfect woman, the kind a man finds only once in his life, and she died, and that's why he can't be with another woman now. Or maybe she died giving birth to a stillborn baby. Or maybe she contracted a disease, some sort of terrible disease, and it disfigured her body and her face before she died, so now he can't bear to look at other women because all he sees before him are her two faces—the one beautiful, the other ravaged from disease, withered. Or else maybe she's waiting for him somewhere far away, waiting faithfully for the man whose booming voice resounds in her memory day and night. Maybe that's why he doesn't give himself over to others, why he doesn't submit to anyone, because he remembers her within himself

more alive than the breath of the women who attach themselves
to him, demanding a piece of his enticing flesh or his thoughts
or both, depending on what they're interested in.

I never thought for example—and it's quite possible—that
perhaps his beloved had been unfaithful to him with his best
friend, and so that's why now he can't bear the sight of a woman.
That perhaps she, who probably had everything, had got bored.
Maybe she had carried on the affair with his best friend for a
long time, and when he realized that every compliment, every
poem, and every truth had all been lies, that he could never
get back everything he had done in those precious years, which
typically happen only once—well, maybe then something had
broken inside him, and now he hates the whole female sex. But
never, I say never, did I imagine that such a scenario was even
possible. I always saw the positive side. That's the star I was born
under, my mother would say to me while I played with my rag
doll on the ship that was taking us from France to America—to
the Promised Land where my father would supposedly finally
realize his dream and his truth to bring us some peace.

"We'll have so much peace and so much money that we
won't know what to do with it," said my father, who saw not a
single lump of gold in California, because he was waiting for
what he believed to be confirmed as truth, to prospect for it. But
if a man waits for a thing to be confirmed, then, more often than
not, it will no longer be of value. All those who've never waited
for the truth to be confirmed actually had the joy of going in
search of it, as we never had the chance to, nor to experience . . .

But what is, just is. Let me return to the subject of meeting Sunny after the philosopher. One night the philosopher was
saying:

"A person doesn't need to be happy to be fulfilled; happiness is not the ultimate aim of all human beings, fulfillment is.
Fulfillment brings with it all that we need in order to confront
things, but it doesn't guarantee happiness; rather, it leaves room
for us to go in search of the truth, and that's the only true path
that in itself is happiness."

Then, without much philosophizing, Sunny replied that he wasn't clever enough to say what he thought, but that he knew the only true path is the one when you find the right woman, together with whom you will be one made of two.

"Are you pulling my leg?" said the philosopher, and they both burst out laughing.

That night Sunny asked me what my favorite game was when I was small.

"Playing house," I said. "I always wanted to play mother to all the children." Sunny looked at me, and in his eyes I saw his vision of wholeness, which seemed to banish my feeling of wasted youth.

Sunny

ANOTHER YEAR PASSED, what to me seemed like only a few hours, and I had long since learned to be happy alone. I had to learn everything differently. To speak differently, to cry, to dream, to be happy, to see differently . . . In fact, in America, I experienced a belated boyhood. As though sensing my masculinity for the first time, as though I had been released from a halter. And I ran without looking in front or behind, as though terrified of wasting my youth and my days in America.

Then, for the third time I met a woman who can tell the difference between the salt of a fake tear and that of a real tear. One who's also learned from experience that there are only a few times in life when the corners of one's mouth truly tremble in the presence of another. And there was no peace within me. At the same time I must sink deeper. There was no other way.

I was with the philosopher late one evening, in a smoky bar, at the time when one's feet disobey one's brain. Her name was Marianne, and she had sparks in her eyes and a flood inside her that would not extinguish any type of fire. It was as though she had been created just for me . . . Of course, at the same time, I knew that this was no ordinary story. But the storyteller who knows the secrets of storytelling, knows the resolution need not be simple; rather, every toss of the stone rolls differently. She noticed at once that I was looking down on her, and that she couldn't win me over, so she began meowing like a cat in heat, wrapping its tail around all my senses, which, naturally, had imagined her naked on the bed. But my senses wouldn't give in to lying down with her just like that, only out of physical need, intensified by the high-pitched trumpets and the powerful piano, which after every song seemingly served up a new wave of music. The next evening, I found myself back there again, with the woman who had no intention of giving up easily on the man who wouldn't submit to her at once—unlike all those before him—and yet who looks openly at her, drinking her in with his eyes and a smile that says: I am a mountain above all other mountains, and no one can climb onto my peak packed with snow, which can be melted with one and only one stroke, but a true one. Because she was no ordinary woman, she saw all that crystal clear. She also noticed that I sensed her eagerness to find that magic wand that would melt the snow; and that I know—as few others do—that, despite her beauty and bravado, until then she had only really been dipping her toe in the shallows, forever seeking deeper waters.

She offered me all sorts of attractions for which all those around me were prepared to pay—and even to overpay. One night I teased her, bringing her to boiling point, and then I just made off, leaving her simmering. Another night, I feigned total disinterest as though she were telling me a load of boring rubbish. I was monosyllabic, leaning with my back against the counter, and with my sleeves rolled up just high enough to reveal the blood coursing in my veins. But it wasn't as simple with Marianne as it was with all the others. She'd find a way to get me to kiss her—for me to want to kiss her, and not for her to kiss me. So one night, when the whiskey was doing the talking and its potency rendered me insensible, I vaguely recall someone dragging me off and carrying me somewhere. I don't know how and I don't know where. I woke up in a yard dotted with trees, as though back home in the woods hearing the nightingale's song. In my half-dream state, my thoughts were carried off to Macedonia, to our woods, to Luna, who was stroking my erection, staring at me with tear-filled eyes. I opened my eyes and I saw Marianne stroking me, the same as Luna. I don't know how she managed to drag me over there, but I do know that that day we sketched the map of passion with our bodies.

The Narrator

AFTER THAT, SUNNY didn't return to the bar for several days. He went straight home from work. He sat with an expression tinged with both happiness and sadness. His mind almost empty of thought. Those days were empty for Sunny. Empty and full. Until the moment he grinned to himself, tossed his cigarette away, and headed back to the bar.

"Hi."

"Hi."

"Why the cold shoulder?"

"I'm here now."

"What do you mean, 'I'm here now?'"

"Just that, here I am, right here."

"You're not here."

"I know."

"What d'you mean, 'you know?'"

"I just do."

"You think I'm just a cheap whore."

"No, not at all. I think you're wonderful."

"Well then, what's the matter?"

"I don't know."

"What do you mean you don't know?"

"I don't know. If I did, I'd tell you."

"You're the most disgusting man in the world, do you know that?"

"Yes, I do."

"Fuck you."

"Fine."

"Fuck you, fuck you, fuck you."

"Don't shout."

"I'll shout if I want to. No one can stop me."

"Fine then, go ahead and shout."

"You'll never see me again."

"I want to see you."

"What do you mean you want to see me? If you did, you would've seen me."

"It's better we see each other tomorrow. I have to go now."

Sunny

THE FOLLOWING NIGHT Marianne showed up drunk, shouting accusations that I was playing games with her, that I was deceiving her with my looks and at the same time tossing her aside like a rag doll, that you shouldn't play games with people that way because no one deserves it, forgetting that she herself had also done the same thing, probably more often and in a more callous way than me. She pounded my chest with girlish fists, shouting at me, after which she grabbed me and lay down on that same chest she'd been pounding only a moment ago, saying: "Don't you get it? I love you."

That's when I felt that I'd shattered what everyone else around me was yearning for. What I'd won and then just tossed aside. What a battle and what a victory! If I went after her, I said to myself, I'd be just like all the others. But this way, because of my commitment to Luna, I didn't go in pursuit of other flesh (dear God, these sinful words of mine . . .). I found a new game that would fill me with delight: attaining the impossible! And I didn't stop there: I caressed her, I looked into her eyes, and promised her that we'd see each other the following day. And then the next day I didn't show up. Mitse told me that he couldn't work me out, but that I could easily play the romantic lead in a film, that everyone was saying I'd become the world's greatest lover. But he didn't tell me that they hated me for the simple reason that nobody can stand anyone that's better off than them, as my father used to say.

But to return to Marianne. After a few days, I showed up at the bar again. She was there. Naturally, she didn't greet me. All her friends waited to see what would happen, not merely feigning disinterest, but acting as if they couldn't even remember what had happened between us. Marianne was standing there, chatting and laughing with an unfamiliar man. She didn't come over to me that night. I made out as if I hadn't seen her, even though, I have to admit, I wanted to know if she wanted to see whether or not I was looking at her. I went home that night in somewhat higher spirits, until the next evening—and several others following it—when she just walked past me with that same man, so close that I could smell them, but she gave no signs she wanted me to know I meant nothing to her, or that she despised me; rather, it was as if I had just evaporated, like her desire and need for me. Naturally, this didn't leave me feeling indifferent.

"A man likes to be dominant. So when the one he dominates over is gone, he's left without the opportunity to satisfy his thirst for vanity. A vanity that's led to countless thirsty people in the world," the philosopher correctly stated, sharing with us a new kind of philosophy from that time, which, once again, I only vaguely understood.

But if I make advances to her, I'll look small in her eyes. A bear doesn't just feed on grass; it needs the honey high up in the tallest tree, which is sweetest only after it manages with great effort to climb the tree, scraping itself and leaving tufts of fur behind on the rough bark, to drink it in forever. By that time, I had already learned to view things from on high, and to calculate them like in mathematics, which, as a child at school, they explained to us with sticks placed side by side, so you could see that one and one make two, and not three or none as sometimes occurs in love. And so, calculating things within myself, like a mathematician who anticipates his own moves and slides his bishop close to the king so that he can take the queen with his horse, I remembered what to do. She was sitting right near me, laughing with her superficial friends, as if everything was right with the world. I went and stood beside the least attractive of her friends, bought her a drink, and then half an hour later left the bar with her. Her poor friend didn't know what to make of my sudden appearance, not realizing that she was just a pawn to be used. Naturally, I had no intention of doing anything with her, and nor did I want to. Then it dawned on me that a monster had been awakened within me whose sole purpose it was to stomp all over everything, just so I could be victorious, like Draga, the woman on the ship, the one that sank, and whose size cannot even be compared to the enormity of my deceit, which had not even been conceived of during the time when Luna and I were creating dreams out of reality.

Marianne had gone looking for us that night, and after she began to cry, she left, saying that she would throw herself into the river as, in fact, she had threatened to do many times before that. The philosopher, who was dead drunk, stopped her. The next day, all he remembered was waking up in a yard dotted with a few trees, as though in a wood.

And I asked the philosopher:

"What did you want with her? What did you both do?"

"I don't know what we did, I was quite drunk," he said.

"What do you mean you don't know; you can't not know."

"Even if I did know, what does that change? Anyway, you don't love her. To you she's just one of many."

"That's true, but she's one of mine, not yours."

"Sunny, you need to grow up and realize that the world doesn't just revolve around you."

"Would you see her again?"

"Yes?"

"Even if that meant losing me?"

"Yes."

"Why?"

"Because nothing matters to me."

"How can nothing matter to you?"

"Just because. Nothing matters inasmuch as everything does matter. But then, if you really want me to, I'll stay away from her. Are you satisfied now?"

"No."

"Well then, what do you want?"

For you never to have gone to her."

"That can never be undone, the same as you can't undo all your past actions. Here, go on then, imagine that you're Luna and that I'm Sunny, and forgive me. That will never happen."

"Oh put a sock in it with that 'imagine, imagine.' You're crazy, man."

"Maybe."

"If you believed in Plato's ideas on love that you spout, you'd never have gone off with her."

"Sunny, do you hear what you're saying? I've told you that I believe in necessity, in closeness, in routine, but not in love. You must have heard me telling you that. I can provide you with hundreds of anecdotes of other philosophers who said the opposite to what they thought. You won't find one truth even in God. People also read him the way they want to."

"Fuck you."

"No, fuck you."

The Narrator

WELL . . . AND AT the same time, far away over there in Macedonia, Luna was like a cowering puppy, sniveling in the corner and only occasionally—rarely—wagging her tail. There was no sunshine for her. She was treated badly both by her own flesh and blood, and by strangers too. Her loved ones just kicked her around. Even her mother. She cursed the day she gave birth to her. "May the milk I suckled you with turn sour; may you vomit all your food; may you have no luck in life for bringing us such shame," she'd say to her.

Her youngest sister didn't want to sleep next to her. Out on the street, people told her that Luna was possessed by the devil, and this made her cry, and she would hit Luna.

"I don't want you to be my sister. Everyone's laughing at me because of you. I don't have any friends because of you. Let my mother give you back to the storks," she said to her.

Her father didn't beat her anymore. Strangely enough, he also stopped berating her. Like a thwarted child, he just quietly averted his gaze and stopped mentioning her name. He didn't want to see her or speak to her again. There was no more conversation at their table. A deafening silence fell over their home.

Luna went often to the pond where she and Sunny had created ripples in the water. Standing before the still water, she uttered the name she would give to the first child that nature would bequeath to them.

She threw stones into the water. And in the ripples formed by the stones she beheld Sunny, and the child. Her blood had already reached new straits and narrows. She started talking to the pond because her other dreams were empty. She gave the baby the name Ray. That's how she looked for and found light. In the dark wells of loneliness and love.

Sunny

ONE AFTERNOON TWO days after our last encounter, Marianne came over to see me. Sober. Because life had taught her that some things can be resolved only by day, when emotions are more often at rest than running high. She called me outside, and lit a cigarette.

"Whatever you do, I will love you my whole life. But if you hurt me like that ever again, no force on earth will prevent me from disappearing forever from this world," she said.

"And the philosopher?"

"What about him?"

"Wasn't he at your place two nights ago?"

"He was. What's that got to do with anything?"

"What do you mean, 'what's that got to do with anything?' What were you two doing?"

"Nothing. He stopped me, gave me a few slaps, we drank some more, and after that he couldn't stand up. Margaret and I took him back to my place because we didn't know where else to take him. He was dead drunk and he slept outside, on the porch."

"That's all that happened?"

"Of course. What were you thinking?"

"Did he sleep where I slept?"

"Yes."

"And you didn't do anything?"

"Of course not."

"How could you let him sleep in the same place I slept?!"

"What difference is that to you? Anyway, you don't care about me? Or do you?"

"I don't."

"Well then why do you care where the philosopher slept? You want everything to revolve around you, Sunny, even the things you don't like. Isn't that right? It pains you even when someone takes something of yours you don't like. Isn't that so? But it doesn't pain you when you're the one doing the taking, eh?"

"You're over-philosophizing."

"You're an idiot, a simpleton who hasn't seen anything in life. You've never deserved anything in life. You have no regard for others. You only take notice of someone if you can get something out of them. You're a selfish jerk . . . Fine, sorry, I didn't mean that. Please, kiss me . . . Can I kiss you?"

"No," I said to her, and that small word composed of two letters hit her like thunder. Her face clouded over. I thought it might sink to the ground. As she was leaving, she gave me a look that a child gives its father after causing some sort of serious mischief and which it thinks it will have to pay for its whole life long. She looked at me in the hope that something inside me had broken, even though she knew quite well how ice cracks . . .

Her look made me regain my dominance, and once again I felt happy. Painfully happy. History, I thought to myself then, is written by the victorious who've won only because they've actually lost.

Luna

Sunny has been gone three whole years. Three years likened to three unborn children; to an unplowed, unweeded field with couch grass, wild untended grass. My body trembles at the thought of him. It—my body, not me—desires his touch, his caresses; to know every part of me, to drink me in, to overpower my gaze, to shame it. My man whose weight was made for mine—it is him it's seeking.

I sleep with his letters. They keep me warm like the early rays after a cold morning spent working in the field. But they don't drench me in sweat as happens when the sun climbs to its zenith, when it ripens just before bursting into bloom. But the soul wants to melt, not to be warmed.

And so I wander around as though headless, as though without protection, without fortification, without anything, something—how can I put it—without . . . without a fire to singe me—yes, that's the right word—without a fire to singe me, so that I can feel alive.

That's how much of my time passes, between the warmth of Sunny's imagined breath and the want of the home fires. Sometimes at night I sit outside with the other women. Now that I'm older, they pay more notice to me. All my friends have disappeared. They just whisper bad things about me behind my back, and spit at me with their eyes whenever they see me. Whereas the men cross to the other side of the street so they don't catch anything bad from me, or else they give me death stares . . .

I've heard all kinds of things on the street—what haven't I heard—everything that up to now I'd heard secretly, because when the women are all alone, their conversation is different. One day I heard Para the troublemaker talking, a neighbor who never zips her mouth, one of those old biddies who's been brutalized by life, and consequently whose soul cries like a ceaseless stream, but who nevertheless has the energy for bold words.

This woman Para, the only one who spoke so brazenly—at that time it was forbidden to speak that way—said to Mitse's wife: "Woman, your husband's been gone a long time. Your legs are trembling; mind some other man doesn't start sniffing around at you, because that might also make you tremble," and she laughed, crazy as a loon. It was shameful for such things to be said or even thought at that time. However, Para was a cheerful, agreeable soul, and both her husband and her son had been slaughtered, killed in the war, either by Serbs or Bulgarians or by one of our own who'd been forcibly taken to fight with them—it was hard to say who was killing whom at that time—and so everyone forgave her.

When she said that to Mitse's wife, my own legs gave way beneath me.

"I haven't seen a man in some time either," I said to myself in my mind. "Does that mean I would also tremble if one started sniffing around at me, and then cry day and night because I was unfaithful to Sunny?" And I wept. Alone every day, I wept tears of sorrow, as though they were letters urging him to come home quickly.

The Narrator

FROM SO MUCH waiting, Luna's nether regions began to stir. One time even seeking out her hand, which shrank back after the touch as if bitten by a snake. Her cheeks turned a red deeper than cherries. Her thing down there spoke to her, as in the past when her underpants had been stained red for the first time; and when, after many years, Sunny made her feel whole. But this time it was different. On its own, unexpectedly, it whispered to her. As if it was crying from loneliness.

Luna strained as if pushing against stirrups. She wanted to cut off her hand. Such an impure thought could only come from the devil, she thought to herself at those strange times. She scolded her thing down there, saying to it:

"Be still. Leave me in peace. Be patient, and don't get all aroused. I don't want to be touched even by my own shadow. Only Sunny has the right to think about me, no one and nothing else in the world does." That's what she said, because the feeling of wholeness within her remained—always—even in the smallest fragments of time. Put simply, Luna was such a perfect image of wholeness, the likes of which not even a mountain presents in spring. In contrast to Sunny, whom she was waiting for with doe-eyed innocence . . .

Ah . . . If there was any justice in this world—even just a drop—then at such a fate, the heavens would open, letting loose a deluge to wipe out all those who have strayed, and to rebuke the Fates, to insist on their decreeing everything differently for both Sunny and her. But when Luna, the poor girl, entered this fallen world, the Fates said:

May a gentle, playful stream that never overflows course through her; may it ice over thinly only in winter, so thinly that it would break were a sparrow to land on it.

The second one said: may her strength come from the heart of a mountain, may it protect her the way the sun watches over the earth. The third drank a bitter potion, and said: all will be

110

bestowed on her as it both should and should not. May the stream flow from the heart of a mountain, and may it mingle with another dream. What it brings to her, we will see from on high. And so it came to pass. The stream was both gentle and playful, albeit mixed with the dirty rain. And from the heart of a mountain, it shot up instead of down, blazing its way over untrodden ground. Even the peak seemed as though it would flood from the heaving rain underground. Until along with the rain there came snow in the middle of summer; and it poured down filthy mud.

After that, however, time spoke, and decreed that Luna's only sin was that she had remained the same person she had always been. Whereas for Sunny in America the words were reversed. And instead of the mountain that gave birth to the purest stream—the one with which he covered himself in bed at night—another would catch his eye in the time to come . . .

But that's how it is, there's no escaping fate. What is written shall come to pass. Were you even to hide inside a bull's horn, it would still find you. The way it found Luna, who will learn that her cherry-red blushes were for a man who had muddied the waters long ago.

Sunny

AFTER MARIANNE, MY desire for Luna began to fade . . .

The Narrator

EXCUSE ME, SUNNY, but I would like to say something.

After Marianne, Sunny's desire for Luna began to fade more and more, sinking even faster, I would say, than the ship that had brought him to America. He had long been aware that if a person chooses the path to the left, the right disappears. Without delay. It was as clear to him as the nightingale's song that his pie would never taste quite the same as before, because he was no longer the same person to taste the same sweetness. He was also aware that, not only could he not avoid buttering his bread on both sides, but he was barely restraining himself from eating the whole thing with relish. He was pained to tears by the fact that from now on—no, not from now; rather, from some time ago, while for Luna it was back even further than that—the ripples that their bodies had once bequeathed to the pond, those perfect circles created by their presence that slowly faded, touching its shores, would never be as they once were. He knew that instead of two ripples in the water created by them there appeared only one. He hadn't been given the power to change things yet. In his mind he already saw just one ripple. Created by one body. His own. Crying was then left without a name.

Sunny

THANK YOU, NARRATOR.

And so what was, sank and faded. Thoughts must now turn to what to do from here on, because time doesn't wait. And if you don't keep moving, you regress, because there's no such thing as standing still. That concept doesn't exist. That's what I tell myself, and I wonder what to think, what to do, what steps to take in this battle with my demons—my proclivities, my penchants, my passions, my pride. What lovely words for such misdeeds. All beginning with the letter "p" . . . Like pleasure . . . And all learned in America. All etched within me as a kind of hallmark dispensed by life to those who've learned much from it. And which remains one's whole life. It can't be erased, setting me apart from others who know nothing of such things, and even from Luna, even from Luna . . .

Ah . . . As I mentioned before, my blessing in disguise was music. It took me far away from those by then familiar dives I went to on nights when I couldn't even stand to be with myself. But believe me, it wasn't just one or two nights. Because from the start I knew that, even if I'd fought against myself with a full-scale military arsenal, being the way I am, I wouldn't win even one small battle, let alone a war. I resolved—or to be more precise—I firmly wished to resolve that I would go only to those places where there was nothing around that could corrupt me. Such a place appeared as if out of nowhere, on a night when the liquor told me that it was over there, and not here. The philosopher and I (yes, yes, we were keeping company again . . .) entered a ramshackle hut made of wood, of hand-sawn, unstained planks of wood, yellowed planks with the knots and the age of the trees from which they'd come clearly visible. Inside, what do I see: a group of black people—all of them black—staring at us in surprise, as if they're saying to themselves, what the hell do these two want in here, what are they doing in our place, defiling it with another color? Even though in those days white people never went to places frequented by blacks, the philosopher spoke to one of the black men, who said something to the others, and then they sat us down at the bar and gave us some whiskey to drink. When a man is best friends with alcohol, then it's as if he's had a falling out with himself, and so nothing seemed as strange as it was to me. Twice that night, a marvel paid me a visit. It appeared with two faces, and twice made me feel reborn. Even though by then I had countless times seen and heard black people sing, everything was different here. First, three or four black women began to sing as though in a trance. Fortunately, I had seen such states of ecstasy as this before, otherwise I might have thought the devil had taken possession of their bodies and was performing a lascivious welcoming dance to hell. The swaying black women were immediately joined by the musicians, each of them with a protruding Adam's apple, as if they were brothers. I don't think I had ever seen such joy on people's faces before. The battered figures with rough hands pricked from cotton—which displays its softness even through its sharp spikes—played such soft music as though it had been plucked from the cotton itself, offering up its softness for us on which to lie down. But not on which to sleep; rather, on which to float like little children, like a child who plays with the father it hasn't seen in a long time. That kind of fervor for their music—which was the same as the music in white people's bars, but which these people played as though born from it, and not it from them—lured me back to their place a few times, even though everyone told me I would have big problems with the people in white robes and hoods.

"They'll cut off your thing, and then you won't have anything to piss with," they said to me.

Mitse said he was worried about me hanging around those grubby Gypsies, who back home we didn't even waste our spit on. He went on at me as much as I remained silent with him, because you shouldn't judge people by their seed but by their fruit, and because everyone has the same color blood, just as everyone's thoughts are their own.

In fact, I'm grateful to Mitse from here to the moon and back, because by telling me about how things should be, he taught me how things shouldn't be. It's not difficult to grasp that he's one of those people who talk more than they act. And from whom, by doing the complete opposite of them, you will learn what, in fact, you should do. Mitse was like almost everyone else in the world. Men who slept with whores were heroes to him. He bought short-lived happiness with his money. His muddy hands were no obstacle to him blowing his weekly pay on women and his so-called friends, who vanished with the last bit of his money. He always dreamed of doing something that had already been done before, and never once dared to imagine or think of doing something uniquely his own, something that was Mitse's, and not a pale imitation of everyone else that had even the tiniest bit of initiative. Even in going to America he had followed in his cousin's footsteps, who was said to be the most successful member of the whole family. Mitse helped out others only when obliged to do so, pulling them out of the mire into which he himself had sunk, tripping up on his own self-created nonsense, but which he claimed someone else had set up for him; or else, when he thought of the possible benefits to be gained by helping someone much stronger than himself—because to him the strong were a bedrock of support on which he could rely, and not a towering height of strength from which they didn't notice him. Mitse wasn't malicious—no, not even in the slightest—but isn't empty-headedness also a form of malice? I don't know, I'm not smart enough to say, but, come to think of it, I say to myself, if you don't direct and divert the water to flow over the seedbed, instead of watering your field, it will flood your harvest, which both spoils from too much water and withers from too much sun. It wants moderation, like everything else in the world. But Mitse knew no moderation. Neither in drinking nor in boasting, not to mention in lying. Whenever the most popular whore in all the bars happened to glance over at him, he would spend the whole week telling everyone that she was his, that she had fallen for him, describing at length everything he would do to her, after which she would supposedly be filled to overflowing, and would never even dream of another man. Whenever he felt like crying, he didn't cry; rather, he just made believe that he wasn't feeling well, that he hadn't slept well that night because he'd been thinking about his family, including his wife, about whom he'd never said a good word when he was living back home or, perhaps more precisely, about whom he'd never said a good word until he left home. What was most interesting about Mitse was that he knew supposedly everything, and he had something to say about almost everything. Poor Mitse had a story for every occasion. He never admitted to his mistakes, or even noticed them. Whatever it looks like in the beginning, such blindness later on reveals itself in the absence of happiness and true friends. And such people begin to live by this or that story, and not by their decisions and actions, and this embitters their lives and prevents them from being who they could have been. What's more, as if by some unwritten law, they tell everyone about their lives, probably because they have nothing else to say, preoccupied as they are with their own fate, which they make no effort to change. Nothing important compelled Mitse to act like a mouse who surrenders in the small hope of having one and only one bite of the cheese it's been licking its wounds for the whole week, in the trap that without fail claps its tail. And nothing really major had happened to him besides having produced a few children . . . But there were many others like Mitse. A majority of others were like that. Only packaged differently.

But to return to the story. As I was saying, at that place, forbidden to my kind, yet at the same time also welcoming to my kind, depending on how one is perceived—or something like that—I met the most remarkable singer in the world. A swarthy old woman, who knew both the sweet notes and the bitter notes, and who produced the finest sounds with her raspy voice. She sang in whites-only bars too. We often encountered her. The philosopher would tell her that she was as wise as an old sage, while I bought her drinks, and called her Majče— Granny in Macedonian—which she laughed at like a child. She tried calling me that too, in broken Macedonian. Majče was a grand woman. Her name was Roxanna. With a heart as soft as cotton—Majče was a mountain, with a heart of cotton—a mountain, from which her cry escaped like laughter, that's what Majče was like. A woman who'd given birth to three white and three black children by four different men, none of whom had been Mr. Right. Majče read palms as well. She told fortunes. She took hold of my palm, ran her finger over the lines, then let go of it, and looked into my eyes instead. In that murky dream state, in which I'm not sure if anything was real, whether everything really happened or not, she seemed to say the following, recounted here in my own words:

"Majče, listen to Majče, you're a sweet child. Don't mind me calling you child; to me you're a child. Soon you'll meet a woman who's not for you. She'll be like a river without a bed, an ocean without a basin. But Majče, believe these old bones of mine when I tell you I know that no force on earth will prevent you from heading into the unknown. Because when you don't know where you're headed, that's when you choose the path that commands your mind and body. And for you that path is the one you're headed down now. Never mind, Majče, never mind, I'm not worried about you because you're one of those people who look upon their scars both with and without fear. However, those scars can't be erased. They'll remain as a gift from your wanderings, from the anger stored within you, and they'll mark you. They'll mark you forever, my dear boy. But such is your path, such is your star, to glide over scars without end. But believe me Majče, all scars are the same, all of them. And if you lack them, it's as if you haven't lived. They're a necessary evil, my dear boy. Now you listen to me—stay here a bit longer, and then go back. It's best you go back to your little home, it's much better there, it always has been. If you heed what I say, you won't make a mistake. I'm saying this to you as a mother would, even though I know your path is not destined to follow my words."

When I encountered Majče's soul for the first time, my heart flew off on its own to Macedonia, to ask after my grandmother, to find out whether or not she had already bequeathed her body to the earth forever more.

The Narrator

WHEN YOU LEAVE traces of yourself in more than one place, then your house becomes divided. Sunny's separation from Luna—the physical one between two countries—was drawing to an end. But he didn't know that. Everything started when, through Majče, he met a new girl. That's when, from out of the dark depths there emerged the points of no return. His winged manhood turned down the wrong road. He stumbled, entering into new expanses. On the wings of abandon.

Sunny

AS FORETOLD BY the dream-turned-reality, through Majče, I met Joanne. She had taken care of her as a young girl, Majče said, and now she too came in secret to hear Majče sing, to the whites-only bars. She looked a lot like Majče. Only, she wasn't so smart. But she was as lively as a wasp, as a whole swarm. It seemed to me that she would start to dance, look me in the eye without lowering her gaze, behave like a mischievous imp, and then just disappear. The way I acted toward Marianne. I wasn't sure what would happen after that. I started going to the bar more and more often. The seasons merged into one another. It began raining out of nowhere. My soul swelled, making room for further mischief. Her eyes hinted at new dimensions, but she never came near me. A flood rose up within me, surging up to my eyes, like a primeval cry. Whenever I bought her a drink, she would take it and then just vanish like a cloud. I was robbed of all strength. Nothing shook her. Nothing ever affected her. I felt like Marianne. I felt just like she did when she looked at me without her gaze being returned. A curse descended from the unruly heavens, and my weak side took over. I had no choice. Somehow, those high cheekbones—on whose curvature a man could wound himself—had to be caressed. I told her that I would transport her to untouched shores, that I would bequeath to her unhurried sighs, and that I would lead her to the center of the whirlpool, but it was all in vain. She just laughed at me. I saw myself in her, and I saw Marianne in me. For the first time the roles had been reversed. I felt what it's like for the shoe to be on the other foot. The blood drained from my face. It turned white. Like the moon in broad daylight shrouded by a cloud. I tried to escape, but to no avail. A chill flowed from my actions, those same ones that were beyond the reach of other women. I climbed steep rises, I trod over undisturbed footprints, I shook strange fruit from trees in dark forests, I howled like an unearthly beast during a full moon, I called out with unfamiliar cries, I rumbled like falling stones, I seized her with gentle hands, while she just looked at me as if I were a snot-nosed kid! I stayed home and tried to think like her, what she would want a man to do for her. Nothing came to mind, because there is no logic to passion. Not a day went by when she didn't spit at me, and run off; fleeing without knowing why, as if chasing her own shadow. And she laughed, as if laughing at the trees because they can't flee their own roots. I caught up to her in a hidden wood. But an embrace didn't ensue in the wild shadows. She hit me. The way my father never did. She rained down a barrage of fists on me; and she laughed once more. I spat blood at her. She gave me bloody looks. And then she disappeared like an unspent storm. The next day I wanted to go see her again.

The Narrator

No, HE DIDN'T go to see her the following day. Or the day after that. He even stopped drinking. He talked only to the water, to the roads, to the crumbs. He dressed in old attire. And then he went out to see New York one last time.

The Narrator

MEANWHILE, MACEDONIA BEGAN feeling the wrath of the Kingdom of Serbs, Croats, and Slovenes. Everyone was being given new surnames. They didn't kick over their tombstones and piss on their graves. But nonetheless, they were besmirching the name of the nation.

"So they've changed your name too, eh Mandža?"

"Yeah, goddamn 'em all to hell, but don't let anyone hear me. My name's Mandžić now. They came around here—may they be wiped off the face of the earth!—and asked me what my grandfather's name was, what my great-grandfather's name was. I told 'em, 'Todor and Goce, that's what their names were.'

"'Well then innkeeper, from now on you'll be known as Todorović, that'll be your name.' That's what they said, and just went off—may God deprive them of bread!—but before they left, they stopped and said, 'Hang on a minute, hang on, you've got a nickname—Mandža, isn't that right? Well then, from now on you'll be known as Mandžić. Forget Todorović, that's too Serbian for you, you fucking Bulgarian.' That's what they said, may they be struck dumb!"

"Boys, I told you that one day we'd all be robbed of our own names. But no one listens to the priest. You all think he's a fool who just prattles on about nonsense. Well, now you know."

"But Father, would it be better if we were all Bulgarians?"

"It'd be better for us to be nothing. That's all I have to say. Because so far we've been this, we've been that, and now look at what we've become. Pumpkin heads, that's what we've become."

"Well then, Father, and what've you ever gotten from being a Macedonian? Is your hat on any straighter than the ones worn by the Serbs?"

"I can live without a hat too. But I want to tell you something else. Shitting on a man's roots is like spitting on their dead. And they didn't look after us for nothing."

"Father, you best shut your mouth. It flaps open too much. Watch you don't swallow your teeth one day, and then wonder why."

"Kole, you best go to your grandfather's grave and ask him if they've restored his tongue up there—the one the Turks cut off."

"Father—my grandfather was a fool. He drank with the komiti rebels in the woods, where they slept like cattle, and for what? To just end up having his tongue cut off. All we ever got from him at home was trouble. Even more so than from the Turks."

"Kole, may God forgive your sins, and others like you. But it seems he has a much more serious job, because no one's ever unshackled us, nor will they the way things are going."

Sunny

AND I SET off once again. I climbed back aboard a ship. Without
wanting to. A feeling of apathy came over me. I didn't feel like
going back home or staying here. I did a lot of thinking on the
ship. It was clear to me that nothing aroused me anymore. Or
scared me. I had no particular desire to see Luna, or any other
woman for that matter. I got bored of thinking. Everything
bored me. I felt as if I'd become lifeless. Quite simply, I didn't
give a damn about anything . . .

I returned to my homeland, which had already begun feeling the wrath of the Kingdom of the Serbs, Croats, and Slovenes.
That poor country, which has always been divided, parceled up
by rogue nations to whom it's been important—as it has been to
me—taking it to satisfy their own needs without considering the
consequences of their heavy hand. My innocent and long-suffer-
ing Macedonia, perpetually in the grip of others because of their
desire—like mine—to suckle from numerous breasts, because
of their desire to absorb everything into themselves—and again
like me—to sap all its resources to water their own fields, not
caring that the people of that land can't raise a crop, or see the
fruit of their labour because of those others, because of those
who wanted everything only for themselves. My homeland was
just like Luna, so to speak. Waiting for its time to come, power-
less to change reality as the others were always stronger than her.
Had that not been the case, had my homeland been more powerful, it probably would have been like the others. It would have
robbed others of their happiness and joy. It would have killed
fathers and men. It would have smashed their teeth in their
mouths, and forced them to swallow their own native tongue.
And it would have raped mothers in front of their children, as is
written that such vile and unimaginable things have been done
to us by other nations. But that story hasn't happened yet, and
there's no need for us to assume it even might. Although, if we
allow ourselves to assume it, we will see that the strong always

exert their brute strength, while those with less strength who rise up against them demonstrate it even more.

But, as I was saying, I returned home, and my first encounter with the neighbors who came out to greet me was like my first encounter with the foreign armies that came to our town during World War I, and took all the men to fight for them; the neighbors saw me the way I saw the soldiers through child's eyes—as someone unfamiliar, strange, with different clothes, and prematurely aged. Only I wasn't taking their men into the army; instead, I gave them small gifts that made their teeth rattle with joy, the way they rattled with fear from all the different armies, be they Bulgarian, Serb, or who knows what else.

Before I saw Luna, my mouth went dry and no voice would come out, which made me as happy as the first time it happened to me, as a child with a piece of bread in my hand. This time, as a grown man with money in his pocket, I won the hand of Luna, whose father cheerfully took back all his previous words, reveling in the shiny pieces of gold that would afford him a year in which, instead of rotting away in the fields, he could boast about his son-in-law in the taverns, after which he would drink the money away, and return to a life of hardship. In those times, that's how people changed the fate of others, their loved ones. Sometimes for the better, but more often for the worse, much worse. And all for the sake of two or three hundred free rakijas in the tavern, and getting up at six in the morning instead of at three.

The Narrator

THE SAME DAY he returned, Sunny went to his grandmother's grave. And for the first and last time he asked her everything:

Did she really know how to count tears?

What did she call joy?

Was it her face or her soul that had aged faster?

What was she like when her face had a different appearance?

What had she shared with her soul before it departed?

On the night I was born, did she pray more or feel great joy?

Did Saint Peter count her poor grievances at the gates of Heaven?

Why almost every day, if my childhood memories serve me right, did she go to visit my grandfather's grave?

In that other world, does Grandfather still have that Turkish bullet wound, and are they now together again up there?

Up there, does he also tell her—as Grandmother used to say—that no one else knew how to make maznik the way she did? And when he says that to her, does she let out a squeal of delight, as she did whenever she recalled it with her hands white from flour—lily-white, the way her fate had never been?

Should I pour two shots of rakija over her grave, as she used to say, so that she can then give it to Grandfather, whom I never saw? Because he would've liked to drink more, but he never actually got to in the course of his life. He just never had the time to.

And how many hardships had she swept under the carpet, shared with no one else in this wide world?

Her grave stood like a rock atop a bare hill, and whispered quietly with the wind. With no one else anymore. The wind repeated his grandmother's words:

"Such is our beastly life: here today, gone tomorrow. And we take everything with us into the ground, as though we had never even existed. Something remains only if you've done some good. It will remain to wind its way somewhere, to let it be known that we weren't here for nothing; and if you've ever hated someone, that will remain too. And a cross. And tears. Nothing else . . . But perhaps, after all, that's no small thing in this spiteful world."

The Narrator

"Hey, Mandža. Oh, pardon me, I meant to say, Mr Mandžić. Why've you gone all pale in the face? Did someone run off without paying the bill, eh?"

"You just sit there and be quiet if you plan on staying. Don't needle me."

"Why? Are you gonna spit in my food if I don't? You'd do it for no good reason anyway, hee, hee, hee . . ."

"C'mon Mitre, quit stirrin' the pot."

"Mandža, go on, stir the pot some more. Ha, ha, ha . . ."

"Right, yesterday you were both ready to kill each other, and come today you're best buddies, goddamned drunkards. What'll you have to drink?"

"Give us what you've got. Some rakija to drink. As if there's anything else to be had. Give us rakija and some salad. Then give us some wine and chicken, that'll do won't it, eh, in-law? Or do you want some ribs? Or should we order some chops, eh?"

"Look here, give us a few chops. Forget that chicken. Chicken's for eating at home, not at a tavern."

"Fine then. And, Mandža, oops . . . pardon me, I've done it again. I meant to say Mr Mandžić. Go on then, ask what the other patrons'll have, so that you can make a little bit extra yourself."

"Oh, Mitre, so you've finally calmed down, eh? Fine, fine. May God grant you good health."

"Hey, Petse, in-law. D'you see what fate's like? A man can never be sure what the day will bring, nor the year. Who would've thought that you and I would ever sit down at the same table? No one. And drink together, no less! But there you have it. And that's come to pass. To be honest, I said to my wife, 'me be that man's in-law, me dance an oro with him, not on your life! I'd sooner dance an oro with mice than with him, that old dried-up rat,' I said to her. Hee, hee. You're not angry, are you?"

"Dammit, me get angry with my in-law? That'll be the day. Well, what didn't I call you as well: a nit, a louse, who knows what else I turned you into. But there you have it—the wedding took place. But forget about all that. What'll we do tomorrow? Patch up holes in our roofs or go hunting?"

"Go hunting, of course. 'Patch up holes in our roofs', he says. They've been gaping so long, dammit, let 'em wait a day or two longer."

"Well then, here's to our health. May our kids give us grandchildren so our family may multiply; and may our grandkids tug on our mustaches."

"Here's to our good luck."

"Cheers."

Sunny

WE WEREN'T ABLE to conceive for quite some time after the wedding. We tried for a whole year and more. In the farthest reaches of the woods, where we'd never been before. We dived into the seedbed of love, split it open, and made a space for it to take root. Together we drank from the wellspring fed by the outpouring of lament for our wasted youth. Everything was the same, and nothing was the same. It was as if a bevy of raw flames surged within us for the first time, sending a different kind of shooting pain down our thighs, a previously unfelt sensation. Luna's eyes showed that something had begun to course within her, to tickle her, to caress her somewhere deep inside and calm her down, like a distant voice from a nearby cave. Then she let out a different kind of moan, and her body pulled away from mine as though it had been scalded.

"What is it," I said to her, "what did I do to you?" while nature all around us revealed that for the first time it had felt the trembling of two bodies in climax, when the earth is moistened with true water.

"Whatever it is, don't stop," Luna said to me. She said it to me with her eyes, because in those times, words were still too shy to talk about such things.

The Narrator

AND SO, LIKE a dream dreamt by all brides, Luna discovered two things on the same day: her body had opened up fully for the first time, culminating in a voluptuous scream that hides in the secret recesses of two bodies. And somehow she felt that a blessing was being born within her, which would also take the edge off the sharp sun.

As the Fates had decreed, a gentle, playful stream coursed through her once again, filling her seedbed with warmth so it wouldn't ice over thinly, and be fragile enough for a sparrow to break through. It shot up instead of down, blazing its way over untrodden ground. And her strength came from the heart of a mountain, and the sun watched over the earth. But what did it matter when the stream had already long ago become mixed with another dream from a dirty sky that had such a terrifying strength, so great, seemingly as though it could grasp the earthly globe and simply crush it.

Sunny

I BUILT A house for Luna and me. In my parents' backyard. A new one, separated from theirs, which was unusual for that time. We slept there, in the calm of expectation.

One morning, amid the calm, the shadows of the past took up residence within me. Showing up like uninvited guests. They sat on my shoulder like a little devil, and greeted me with a false kiss.

I began waking up in the new house to the Macedonian nightingale's song. In my half-dream state, my thoughts flew off to our nearby woods, to Luna, who was stroking my erection, looking at me with eyes that seemed to well up with passion. Sweetness filled my veins. My eyes closed and opened again to a different dream where, instead of Luna, another woman with milk-filled breasts was stroking me! I felt a sense of warmth in my groin. My dream shifted, and I saw the smile of Marianne's pregnant belly. Out of nowhere, Joanne appeared too. She lay down beside Marianne, and stroked her belly. The four of us sank into a blissful dream.

Luna broke my dream, shaking me awake.

"You were calling out a woman's name in your dream. You're sweating. You're soaking wet. Let me bring you some new clothes to change into," she said.

As she was getting me some clothes, I saw that my manhood had stirred to life because of another woman; my manhood that didn't want to settle down, and which, that day, that morning, didn't want to attend to Luna. Instead, it subsided confusedly into far-off desire.

The Narrator

It's AS IF there's not a soul in this world who's remained faithful to the original truth. It seems people change like the wind. They say one thing one day, and something different the next. You can't rely on anyone. Such a time is upon us.

Sunny

WHEN I WHISPERED my sweet nothings to Luna's breasts, when we shared our secrets with one another, it made the heavens blush bright red. And with a final breath before the storm, the heavens sent a bolt of lightning to strike the center of the field, with no regard for what it struck. Then the touch was not permitted earthly gravity. Nor the lips a hint of expectancy. It was all like that, just as I'm describing it, everything was like that, but only while I was whispering to her breasts, to her body. The rest of the time, it was as if my dream was filled with Marianne and Joanne; the wretched dream was like a long-distance messenger, sent to prod me, and to remind me that I wasn't born to follow the straight and narrow path.

The story continued as though sprinkled with wormwood. And after a brief flicker, that little smile I had dissolved.

Luna, encouraged by the freedom we'd allowed ourselves in that tempest, by the freedom of our small house, in the times when people from our parts had never seen a naked woman—not even the men their own wives, because it was shameful—well, at such a time, in the morning, Luna would call me in her fairy-like voice to marvel at her breasts, heavier than ever before from the milk being produced by her . . . Poor simple-hearted Luna . . .

As for me, on the other hand, as time went on, as her belly grew, my hands became at odds with one another, as though one belonged to me, and the other to someone else. One hand reached for her breasts, stretching toward those ripe melons as if seeing them for the first time, while the other hand hesitated as though in two minds, as though tasting an old sweet. Luna seemed to see the signs.

"Sunny, have I done something wrong to you? Have I said something to offend your mother, or have I been rude to your father? May I be struck down if I have. Have I looked askance at someone? May my eyes melt if that's the case. Am I not sweeping up the yard properly? Am I not preparing the food the way you like it? . . . " asked Luna.

I didn't know what to say to her. One day, I sat down at the table and Luna served me salted meat, the type that cures for several months in an autumn barrel, and which in winter you can hardly wait to try. For those first few days, and even months, the meat is tasty—extremely so. It's almost as if you had forgotten how to smack your lips together, as though you were doing it for the first time. But spring was approaching, and at the close of winter you feel like tasting fresh meat; the salted meat becomes chewy, and you don't want to put it into your mouth. That day I saw Luna as the salted meat; she seemed to me like last year's leaf, like stale water, or sampled rakija. And I threw the glass against the wall.

PUT SIMPLY, SUNNY couldn't explain himself at that time. He didn't realize that he'd encountered boredom. And that it had now become his biggest enemy.

*

After his hands, Sunny's eyes became at odds with one another. And his looks. And in the end his mind split in two. For the first time, there were days when he felt no desire for Luna. He stared at her when she took him in her hands, but instead of gathering strength—even from the earth—he stood there drooping like a withered tree. His smile left him, it just dissolved. To be honest, at times he just went through the motions because that's what's done, not because his soul compelled him to . . .

Not that he didn't desire Luna. His manhood responded to her presence even from afar. But his mind had changed, a vein it seems had burst, and he had become a different person, dammit. A different Sunny, who it appears cannot walk a straight path in life.

*

Their shared passage was no longer viewed through rose-tinted glasses, tainted by dirt that could not be wiped away.

First, Luna's smile began to annoy him. The same one that as a child he longed would lovingly pass over him. It was as if she were laughing both when she should, but also when she shouldn't. That's how his two eyes, at odds with one another, perceived it.

"Move your hand. You're making me hot," he began to say to her at night, when he started covering his soul with an icy sheet.

"Stop stroking me like that. Be more gentle," he began to say to her, unlike before when he thought that only she knew how to stroke him so gently, the way the horse chestnut strokes the ground in autumn.

"Don't chew like that," he'd say to her, staring at her mouth, the same one from which as a child he waited to hear what kind of sweet words might emerge to endow the first boy in the street with wings.

"Speak, say something," he'd say to her. And the timid Luna began to fear she might say something uninteresting. She began second-guessing herself, composing her thoughts before saying anything. And she talked less and less.

"Can I have a bite of your bread?" she asked him once, in the hope that he'd reply with the first words that didn't presume what kind of fate lay ahead.

"No," he said to her.

Her pregnant belly seemed saddened by that "no."

"Come and feel the baby kicking, as if it's a boy," she'd say to him.

"Make sure it is a boy," he'd say to her.

"Sunny, I can't lift up the water jug. Can you bring it to me?" she'd ask. "Right away," he'd say, and she would wait patiently for that "right away" that didn't eventuate immediately, and that turned into loneliness.

Poor Luna thought to herself:

"I've heard it said that a pregnant woman is like mutating cholera, that her thoughts are constantly changing, that one thought leads to another. And that she will see things that never were. That's what the old folks say. I've also been beset by such cholera. I must make sure Sunny doesn't see it," she would say to herself, and plastered on a few fake smiles. She became more and more jovial, and more and more insignificant.

THEN, FOR A short while, time veered off its track. It became circular like Luna's sweat-soaked belly, which it caressed, and the seed slid propitiously from her womb. Ray came into being. His voice struck the air, his eyes perceived its radiance, his body sensed the closeness of another human being. Ray, the child whose name was borrowed from the sun, began the eternal cycle of parting and reunion. The Fates, from whose decrees there is no escape, seemed angered that night. This is what each of them said:

A different fate awaits this child; may he glide through it like a fish, but may he also bear wings. And may he decide whether he will fly high or dive deep down.

The second one said: on his twentieth summer, may he shoulder a pack and go in search of the truth, and from there a mountain peak; may he reduce the peak to the size of a stone, may he flatten it, and may he look right through it. Let's see what he sees.

The third one said: may he discover all the colors of the spectrum, may he combine them, may he have the power to see even the tear of the queen bee; and may he search farther and deeper, in the shadow of a dream, and in the dirty rains.

And so it came to pass. In summer he was visited by snow, and in winter sweltering heat. Like all travelers.

*

Ray had many journeys in his life. The first began when his father left home, even before he got to know him by the way he breathed. The other began when he himself left home.

Sunny

I CAN'T TELL her. What do I say to her? That I no longer desire her? For that one sentence to give rise to a thousand doubts that would break fragile Luna, break her like a dry twig off a tree in spring, after which it bakes and scorches in the sun all summer long, alone and unprotected. No, I can't do that. And even though by not saying anything I'm still lying, I won't tell her the truth. A lie doesn't hurt, but the truth does, I said to myself, despising myself once again for becoming even worse than my father, and everyone else I know.

Then I began staying out late in bars. Like my father . . . When Mitse came back, I started hanging out with him. Instead of coming home on time, we stayed out drinking together, recounting our time in America. He almost cried from nostalgia about how good it had been over there—the same as he used to do about Macedonia when he was in America—and he also boasted that over in America he'd made the women tremble, after which they wound around him like kittens, little realizing that everyone around him knows his feet shake from uncertainty, which carries him like a spring stream carries a leaf. For my part, I just recounted stories that had nothing to do with any women at all. I told Mitse that if he said anything, I'd tell his wife everything, and I was vindicated on that score.

Mitse started associating with the Serb officers. He began speaking broken Serbian, spending all his money on buying them drinks at the bar, while his wife, like many times before that, cursed the day she had first laid eyes on him.

"You . . . you're—how do I say it—you're a nation. Congratulations to you! May the milk you drank from your mother's breast be blessed," he'd say to them. And they'd say:

"Buy us another round, Mitse. You'll be a true Serb one day, not like these uneducated people of yours." Mitse's teeth would rattle from joy, because he'd finally be something, not the nothing he had always been.

"Well now, Mitse, instead of becoming an American, you've become a Serb, what's all that about?" our people teased him at the bar.

"Don't talk so much. I've always been, or how should I put it, I've always felt myself to be a Serb. My grandfather was a Serb, and so am I. You'll be one too, believe me. And all of you others here who are laughing. If not, you'll cop a beating from the officers and the military police. They'll make mincemeat out of you," Mitse said.

"Well now, you've switched to the Kumanovo dialect spoken by Serbs, Mitse. You're a learned one, you know all the languages," they said to him, teasing poor Mitse.

"Go on, talk. You just talk. My time'll come, and yours'll be gone," Mitse would say.

During that period, for the first time Luna asked me why I mixed so much with him. And for the first time I hit her, and told her not to ask unnecessary questions.

Nevertheless, when Ray came into the world, I went back to my old self. Everything was new to me. A child cries, it won't let you sleep, there are obligations and delights, and somehow I forgot everything. But low tide lasts a short time in a choppy sea. With every revolution of the sun and the moon, the water yields to the shore's pull and it enters and merges with the land. And you have to emerge from that endless cycle to see how the sun—just one step behind that interplay of two forces of nature—has created dry land or hard rock or helped trees, grass or be it whatever else grow.

And when Mitse told me that he'd go back to America again, my thoughts bloomed like an early morning flower, caressed by the sun. But I said no. I closed the flower by force. I brought darkness to it at once to make its petals sleep as if nothing had happened. But to no avail. A flower has only to see the sun once to dream of it the whole time, wanting more than anything to open up. If necessary, it would even fashion a sun out of the earth, just to draw the rays with full force. Like me, who sat, waited, and rejoiced. I'll say it again, it's not as if I wasn't glad; I was a happy man, only at the same time I was also unhappy. When my son turned two, the thirst within me swelled up like a spring after heavy rain, and I think it crushed all the stones lying around, even those that it never managed to get wet in the years gone by.

I dreamt, ardently imagining Luna—my one and only, but also my wise one—looking into my eyes, and speaking to me the way I do, the same as me, giving me all the details I wanted to hear. But they will never be uttered, simply because no one thinks like that, because they shouldn't think like that. Or then again, maybe they should, but there's no one in the world like that who would have the strength within to struggle to create what I wanted to be created. I dreamt, ardently imagining Luna telling me everything I wanted to hear, and releasing me from everything so I can return free, because people have to free themselves in order to be free. And in the dream, speaking through my desire, and releasing me with a firm look in her eyes, she says:

"Go, if you must go. Do what you think necessary to bring down the wall around your heart. Flee far from yourself, run fast like the clouds, but watch you don't stumble on level ground, and that you don't abandon yourself. There, try to heal from what you have lived through, from what it is that turns you upside down at night, from the fact that the touch of my breasts makes you go limp, from whatever it is that has cast a pall over your eyes and stolen the gleam with which they once looked at me. I'm not interested in what once was or what will be. I know that you will come back. That you will always return. That's enough for me. Nor am I asking you to cry out to the late-night moon to retrieve what once was, because what was can never be again, and what will come we have to earn by helping each other. I chose this card from the deck and I'm not afraid that I will lose this game. I'm more afraid that I will lose you if I don't let you go. You're like the wolf: if you tie it up, it will gnaw its own foot off to escape. Don't gnaw at your soul. Go if you must go, but come back. Come back. Don't ask me if someone has told me something—I've heard nothing from anyone. I only heed the glow in your eyes, but they've lost the twinkle they once had. You're a live fire and light water. You need to burn and to swim. And I know that man isn't born to carry such contradictions within himself, and that's why I say to you go. Either put out the fire, release the water, or unite them in some magical way, if at all possible at some point and in some place. I'm here for you. Always. I was here also during the time of our brief spring, and when our summer suddenly darkened over like winter. I'll be here and I'll wait for you, perched atop an autumn leaf, with a lump of snow in my heart and with spring tears welled up in my eyes, reddened from crying. But that's not important. I'm happy no matter what situation I'm in. Even when I'm deathly unhappy, I'm happier than anyone else I know, simply because of the fact that in this brief existence of ours—which would kill even a strapping big man, and I'm not a strapping big man—I met you. I never deceived myself into thinking that everything would be the same. I sensed that long ago, ever since I wanted to stroke the first sign of your beard, which to me seemed beyond reach, farther away than the sun, but which I recognized perfectly after your return, when I saw the shadow of your beard for the first time. You did something for me that no one has ever done. You made me feel like the only woman on earth, and I must make you feel like the only man. I know that I made you a special person, but the star I was born under granted me the desire to give more than to receive. Your son will be just like you. That makes me even happier. I hope that he will make some other woman—who has yet to set foot on the stairs of uncertainty—feel as though she's one of a chosen few in this whole wide world, chosen to feel and to experience what I was able to have with you. I pray that she does the same for him in return, because if a person isn't aware of his own uniqueness—if indeed he has it—he remains unhappy and goes through life like a rag doll. You are too good a person. Yes. Whatever you attempt to do that goes against your beliefs, you can't go through with it. You're a fighter in constant battle, and you can never win. That must be painfully difficult. I don't want to see you struggle until your weapon goes blunt and you have to throw it away like a piece of scrap iron, because a man without a weapon is no longer a man. I love you my soldier, even though the frontlines are many, while you are just one. I don't want to condemn you to a lost battle, even if it's a way for me to hold on to you. I don't need a defeated fighter. I know that a fighter holds on to his spark until he's completely drained, until he wins the battle through many wounds. I don't want to see you as a mountain that on the one hand teems with life, while on the other—from the shadowed side—struggles with some kind of rare, dank moss. Your challenges lie farther away. My path is smooth, and yours is not. If we want to walk together, we must leave our paths as such—separate, but close together, side by side, so that we can call to one another from afar, and catch one another's scent from up close. No one should ever pull another onto their own path. All they'll get is someone identical to them, and from two they will become one, which isn't worth a single thing, let alone two, as they taught us in school. So for that reason, go, with me in your thoughts and with Ray in your mind's eye. Go, carry us within you. In any case, we will wait for you. Don't delay too long. Every year takes something from your life, and we don't have very much. No one in this world is that blessed. I want you not to forget that I know what every one of your marks of ink on paper are even as you form the words in your thoughts. I know where your words falter, and where they don't. Your words are hesitant, but true. The fact that they don't speak the whole truth doesn't bother me. I know it's not right for a person to think like that, but the star I was born under granted me the desire to give more than to receive. To some that's a curse, to me it's not. Remember, fearful trembling sometimes becomes overpowering, but that's not a sign that you've finally lost the battle. There is a lot of strength within you. You carry the strength of the whole male race, but you can't remain on one course. Don't worry; I've never doubted you or myself, not even for a single moment. I never doubted that we wouldn't do all that we had to do. You and I are a symbol of eternity, a tree that stands in the middle of the road, if that's what it believes it must do. Don't push it aside. I give you your freedom that you can even take for yourself, but then it wouldn't be freedom for you. Nevertheless, the freedom given to you is the result of your own desire, and I give it to you because the star I was born under granted me the desire to give more than to receive. Go, and come back. It's true, my most vibrant eyes are no longer the liveliest. And yes, that's the result of your absences too, but not only because of them. The passage of time also brings you wrinkles, but they make you even more handsome. The premature gray hairs in your head and your beard are a gift from the gods to make you look wiser and more masculine, to make you look stern and authoritative, though, in reality, you're a man who often needs support. Your essential battles aren't lost in advance, purely because you are a good person. That is your main characteristic, which makes you irresistibly unique. A characteristic that I'm certain you will hold on to your whole life. That's why I'm letting you go with an easy heart. Not that there won't be any further shadows that fall across my eyes. Not that I won't stop searching for you in the darkness, huddled in bed every night, grabbing hold of a corner of the blanket with both hands. And not that I won't stare into the dark distance, together with that cursed but familiar feeling of happiness tinged with sadness, because of the thought that I have you forever, but won't have you in the countless future revolutions of the sun and the moon. True, I'll feel pity and sorrow for you, and our house will resemble a field covered over with frost, with its silent tears. And I'll get scared, even though I say I don't get scared. I'll tremble with fear from the never-ending time spent without you, even though I'm sure that you'll come back, that you'll always return. Even the droplet is sure that it will nestle in the cloud its whole life, but it cries whenever it goes off to join the great oceans. And its path through the mountains to the clouds seems very long to it, without end. But it's the same path as that of the husband and the wife, and they always end up together—the cloud, the droplet, the husband, the wife—if they want it badly enough. You and I still have a lot ahead of us. For us to go on, you must fly, spread your wings, and free yourself from the desire for flight, which I know will always be with you, because you—and that's why I love you—are someone who soars high, who knows how to fly, and who is sometimes afraid to fly and wants to remain firmly on solid ground. I love you and all those things about you. I love you both when you make out to be strong and when you really are strong. You allow me to see the thing I love as it really is, and not how I think it should be. And because of that, in this life I don't have to deal with the feeling of imperfection, which makes people's lives miserable and unhappy, all just because of the fact that they can't have what they once had, little realizing that they would still have whatever it once was if they just let it be as it was. You gave me the freedom to find that out, to retain that insight deep within me, which warms me the same way Ray does when he's lying on me, and we're breathing with the same rhythm, as one, and not as two. Go, but first kiss me like a king his slave girl and like a man his lover and like a husband his wife. Kiss me the way you know now in this moment, because your kisses aren't the same once you've left, they're not the same anymore. I'm not the kind of woman who has reconciled herself to imperfection, and who is looking for a way to justify her unhappiness. No. I'm a woman who is very well aware of how swollen water washes away the support of trees with shallow roots, and that's why I don't allow my branches to touch the ground. Instead, I let my leaves drop, some falling in autumn like the end of a song, others, plucked by force by a strong wind, and scattered prematurely, before they get to see all the sparrows singing to their true loves. So again I say to you go, and don't fear the waves. They're tall only for those who are small. And you are both tall and small, but when you're small you're also tenacious, because you know the secret paths of both the bees and the wasps. You will leave us like a wolf and like a cub, and you will return like a lion and like an eagle. I'm sure that you will return, that in no time your path will veer off and lead you back here. And awaiting you will be the vicious circle through which you will endlessly turn, in good times and in bad, laughing and crying. For while we are here, we will see everything and ask everything, and you and I, after everything we do and everything we find, will invent some sort of protection from every hardship, of this I'm sure, because this privilege is given to only a few, a privilege spoken about since the time of the first written word. Wait, let me look at your face, let me remember every part of your body, let me touch you in all the places that I know as I know myself, let me remember your hair whose every strand I could even give a name to, as though everything of yours were my own offspring. That's how well I know you, and that's why I miss you so much when you're gone, but also why I'm filled with you when you're not here."

There, that's what I wanted Luna to say to me, for both honey and milk to flow through my soul, but Luna couldn't think on such a level, or even imagine such a thing or know such words . . . The poor thing, she simply loved, that's the kind of person she is, simple in her love, and spirited in showing her love. In a word, perfect. At least to me she is. It's a pity that she came across me, a dud, a failure, who's been given everything, and to whom nothing is enough. Poor me.

Ray

I GREW UP alone. Not alone, but without a father. At the age of eighteen—at the end of 1944—I went off to fight with the partisans. There was no one to tell me not to go. Well, that's not quite true. My mother, Luna, told me not to go, almost tearing her hair out, so to speak. But, as I was saying, there was no one to tell me not to go. I don't know why I went off with them. I followed orders, I did what I was told. I was obedient. Unlike at home, where you could say I hardly ever obeyed. The war ended. It ended quickly. I didn't have a scratch on me, but I carried a few letters across the front line, apparently important letters, and like that, without a scratch on me, they gave me a medal. They gave me a medal for no reason, you could say. So many men died at the front, dear God, so many men died; so many saw their friends left without arms, without eyes, without legs, with their guts spilled out, and the convulsed expressions on their faces that knew they had only seconds left in this world. And how many of them, dear God, how many were there who were left without arms, without eyes, without legs . . . Most of them got nothing out of it at all. Most of them. All they got were their dreams at night. Their dreams that made them wet themselves like children, lying in bed with the women, who, naturally, didn't want a piss-weak man. Such was my luck—the country needed young heroes, those who hadn't sprouted whiskers yet, as they say, and they found me. How they found me I don't know, but they did, and I brought home a medal for my mother. The poor thing melted from joy. She melted from joy like never before, or like I'd never seen before.

In 1950 they sent me to Zagreb, to a university, so I could return home, back to Macedonia, to work for the good of the country. From my first day there, I wasn't interested in the good of the country or the university.

"You have a medal, so you need to study as much as five men put together," the teachers said to me, while I said to myself, if it's all about the medal, then let the medal study, let the medal do the learning if it's that important. And I repeated semester after semester at university. I wrote reams and reams of formulae, and my very long, my overly long stay at university, was just long enough to drink up my youth, just long enough to drink up my youth. There I met Nena. I met her, but it might have been better not to have met her. Or then again, maybe meeting her and not meeting her would have been the same thing. Because the end is the same for everyone, as is the beginning, while the middle depends partly on the circumstances, but above all on the person, who, be it whomever he meets in life, will be unhappy or, if he's happy, will be unfulfilled, which sometimes is the same as being fulfilled. And what can one do in such a world? All that remains is to drink. There's nothing else. Nena didn't believe in anything either. Neither in God nor the Party nor authority. She didn't even believe in herself. She believed in nothing. Maybe that's why things were easier for her. Much easier to have everything she wanted. Whatever she desired. Whatever she imagined having. And because she was beautiful, of course. In that everything of hers, I occupied a special place. A place that probably finished me off. Not that I'm angry. If not for that, it would have been something else.

Nena always showed up at my place on the days she was depressed. When the nothingness inside her was so big that she couldn't stand it anymore. She would tell me that I was too good, and that I was the only genuine person she knew. After that she would run off. She would flee. She would leave. After that, she would go off along her own path only to return to my place once again. And I was always here. Not that I was waiting for her. I wasn't waiting for anyone. Nor did I feel the need to wait for anyone. I was simply here. I couldn't even get rid of her when she came. I felt such a devotion to her, that is to the rare occasions when she showed up at my place as though battered by the spring rain, with dozens of scars that have left their traces, visible traces.

And in this way, years of study passed. To stay in Zagreb— not because of Nena—I enrolled in a different university. I have a medal, they have to accept me. And give me a scholarship. That'll allow me not to have to work, but to drink. That'll allow me to drink up my youth, which doesn't mean anything to me. Youth, such as it is, will pass by in one way or another.

The sixties were approaching. Nena and I liked to drink at the local pubs. And from afar, from quite far off, we caught wind of the sounds of freedom from the West, the freedom from the West that would later prove to be as hypocritical as our own social reality. But whatever you do, without exception, you always have to choose between two evils. You always have to choose between two evils, without exception. So we opted for that second one, the new one. There, in one of the pubs, in a haze of drunkenness, a man with a beard and long hair appeared, wearing a cowboy hat. He always spoke as though he were spouting philosophy. That man spoke about learned things. He said that he was from these parts, but that he wasn't born anywhere, that's how he felt, he said. He knew how to speak Macedonian too, but he was a man without roots, he said, while we, who did nothing but trip over our roots, listened to him, because he wasn't like the others. As I was saying, he—the man with the cowboy hat—said that every man must search in life, he must seek in order to see that he will never find anything. But if through experience he doesn't learn that he will never find anything, then he is nothing. Because the search for nothing turns whatever that nothing is into something, but only because you're searching for it. There was only one thing he hadn't found out, he said: he didn't know what was worse—infidelity to one-self or to another. That's what he said, and we listened to him like a teacher who'd learned everything in life, seeing him as a rare genuine man, and we were grateful to him, because he gave us strength, the strength to feel as though we weren't alone in this world.

He was suspicious at first, a little old man, around sixty years old, without anyone to call his own, mixing with us young people. But he paid for our drinks, so I put up with him. He bothered me too because he resembled me somewhat. We had the same noses, and he was very smart, and also because Nena looked at him the way she looked at me. After a while, he stopped bothering me, but he also stopped interesting me. After a short time he himself had nothing new to tell me. He said that when a person is in search of nothing, he should just take care not to hurt those who aren't in search of nothing, but who find themselves on the same path as him who is searching for it. That sounded funny to me, because how would a person who'd reached such heights be together with someone who isn't searching? Then, one day—one night to be precise—among the dozens of drinks we consumed on his tab, when I no longer knew whether that guy over there was the one with the cowboy hat, he came over, he approached me, and said:

"I'm going now. I'm leaving. These past few years I've lived in order for you to . . . Oh, it doesn't matter. Nothing matters," he said, and he made as if to embrace me. But I pushed him away. I wanted to stomp on this poor old man, to beat him up, to make his blood spurt out while he was down on the ground, to step on his face, to wipe the smile I never saw off his face, to make it disappear the way it never appeared on mine my whole life, and after that for them to separate me from him, only for me to go up to him once more and finish him off, to make him spit dark blood. That's what I wanted, but I just gave him a shove and let him leave, because it doesn't matter. Because nothing matters inasmuch as everything does matter.

About the Author

DEJAN TRAJKOSKI is a writer and journalist from Macedonia. He is founder and director of the International literature festival PRO-ZA Balkan, and a member of the editorial board of the film magazine *Kinopis*.

About the Translator

PAUL FILEV is a literary translator. His most recent publications include Sasho Dimoski's *Alma Mahler* and a groundbreaking anthology of contemporary Macedonian fiction, both published by Dalkey Archive Press.